DIAMOND IN THE ROUGH

BRENDA JERNIGAN

CONTACT - bkj1608@juno.com

WEBPAGE - www.brendajbooks.com

❀ Created with Vellum

QUOTES

"Heartwarming and fun, Diamond in the Rough is a feel-good read guaranteed to delight. Brenda Jernigan writes stories full of hope, humor, and the power of love. Read one of her books and you'll become a forever fan."

~ Sue-Ellen Welfonder, USA Today bestselling author

DEDICATION

This book is dedicated to Bonnie Gardner for being there at the beginning and to Sue-Ellen Welfonder for proofing and helping me to get the book released.

And to Paige Wheeler for loving Devon.

INTRODUCTION

Long time ago in a land before cell phones
& internet, TSA & political correct,
lived a young woman named Kathy
Taylor. She was rather plain and did not
have a lot of confidence, but she had
one hell of a personality.... This is
Kathy's story....

CHAPTER 1

"*T*he hell you say!"

The man standing on the front porch looked a little surprised by the young woman's outburst. "I--I beg your pardon."

"This is a joke, right?" Kathy Taylor leaned out the door of her New Orleans apartment. She glanced left and right, then finally her gaze rested again on the short man in front of her. "Who put you up to pulling my leg?"

"I assure you, Miss Taylor, I'm very serious. I represent Dudley, Smith and York." He glanced down at the papers held in his hand. "And I'm sorry to inform you that your Aunt Catherine Dubois has passed away and has named you as her heir." The messenger shuffled his feet and cleared his throat before continuing. "Mr. York, her attorney, has asked me to convey his condolences and to inform you that you've been left a good sum of money. I'm sorry if I startled you earlier."

Trying to comprehend what the little man in the brown suit had just said, Kathy Taylor rested her shoulder against the doorway. She was going to be rich? Something didn't sound quite right, and why hadn't her mother told her of Aunt Catherine's demise? "It's not every day someone gives me news like this. What am I supposed to do now?"

He reached inside his coat pocket. "This is Mr. York's business card." Handing her a white card embossed in gold, a look of relief washed over his face. "Just call and make an appointment. Mr. York will be glad to fill you in on the details."

Kathy's sturdy fingers reached out for the white paper. She held it in front of her and read the bold, impressive print: *Devon York, Esquire.*

"Can I tell him you'll be calling?"

She glanced back. The messenger looked absolutely miserable as beads of sweat trickled down his face. Kathy had the feeling if she didn't agree he would remain on her doorstep forever. Sighing, she said, "I'll make an appointment Monday."

"Good day, Miss Taylor." The older gentleman turned and walked slowly back to the limousine parked at the curb. The whole thing reminded Kathy of the old television program, "The Millionaire." Of course, this man hadn't handed her a check for a million dollars. She stared after his retreating figure, still disbelieving what he'd just told her. Rich! That only happened in movies -- to *other people* -- not her.

She shut the door and leaned against the smooth brown wood. Cool air wafted across her body. "Thank God for air conditioning!" This was only June, and if the temperature were any indication of what this summer held, New Orleans would be unbearable. She moved toward her blue velvet, sectional couch. Before plopping down, she grabbed a handful of malted milk balls and popped one into her mouth.

Savoring the flavor of malt, she thought of Aunt Catherine. Kathy had never cared for her aunt, and she really didn't know why. Perhaps it had to do with the fact she was named after her. When Aunt Catherine visited she had constantly hugged and kissed on her, which was embarrassing. Kathy could even recall the sweet scent of her perfume. And when she had begun to gain weight, her aunt had constantly harped. She could hear her now, "You're turning into quite a butter ball, young lady."

Popping two more chocolates into her mouth, Kathy mumbled between bites, "Did she think I lugged around this extra fifty pounds because I liked it?"

Kathy couldn't remember when she was thin. The weight just seemed to have crept up on her. Yes, it was true she loved to eat. But the problem, as her sister Tina liked to point out, was that Kathy was an emotional eater. If that were true, Bill was the problem she'd tried to eat away.

William Deveraux Smythe had been dashing, debonair and attracted to her. Yes, she had fallen hard. Three years had passed and still the hurt lingered. After their emotional parting, she'd promised herself she would never let her guard down. Love just hurt too much. It wouldn't happen again.

The door rattled, then swung open, bringing a halt to Kathy's reflecting.

"Is this all you've done today? Sit on the couch and stuff your face with candy." Tina entered the front door with her arms full of bags and packages.

Kathy flipped her brown hair over her shoulder, and cut her eyes to the ceiling before sliding off the couch to help her sister. Sometimes she wondered if Tina ever had anything good to say . . . especially to *her*.

"I've cleaned the apartment while you've apparently

bought out the stores." Kathy took two parcels and followed Tina to the bedroom.

"I assure you, I need everything I got. Remember, I'm the one who received a promotion. Besides, Eric and I are going out to the country club tonight."

Kathy tossed the boxes on the bed. "You're dating that gorgeous hunk you went out with last week?"

"The very one." Tina grinned like a Cheshire cat.

Kathy opened the Saks Fifth Avenue box and pulled out a royal blue, silk dress. "Wow! This is beautiful, Tina. I imagine this set you back a pretty penny."

"Eric's worth it." Tina stood at the mirror brushing her long, silky blond hair before sitting down at the dressing table.

Kathy watched Tina, wishing she had her sister's good looks. Tina's golden hair and blue eyes definitely proved blonds had more fun. In this family, Kathy had gotten the short end of the stick.

She looked at her reflection over Tina's shoulder while she primped. *What a mess!* Kathy thought as she stared at her image. She picked up the brush and ran it through her hair. Why couldn't she have had golden hair instead of mousey brown? And why couldn't she have been tall and thin instead of five foot two? Okay, let's find something positive, she told herself as her sister rattled on about her shopping trip. That was a hard one. Let's see . . . she had high cheekbones, but they were hard to see because of her fat chin. How about eyes? Kathy opened her lids wide to take a good look. They were definitely an unusual gold color with tiny dark brown specks, but she couldn't see a damn thing without contact lens. She shrugged at her image. Well, at least she had one hell of a personality, and one day someone was bound to discover that fact.

"Kathy . . . Kathy!" She saw Tina had stopped brushing her hair and sat staring. "You've not heard a word I said. And what's so funny?"

"Oh, nothing . . . just a private joke."

"Are you going out tonight?" Tina asked.

"No." Kathy turned away from the mirror. "I'm fixing a big pot of spaghetti, and I rented the movie, "Beethoven." I've been dying to see it."

"Yuk!" Tina frowned. "Well, it's your life, but you shouldn't stay cooped up in here all the time."

That might sound fine and dandy for someone who has a date, Kathy thought. But it was useless trying to tell her sister how she felt. Then she remembered her earlier visitor. "By the way, Aunt Catherine died."

"I know, Mother told me last night."

Kathy stopped at the door and looked back at her. "Well thanks a lot for letting me know," she said before walking out of the room.

"I didn't think you'd care," Tina called out. "She never was your favorite person." There was a pause before Tina's footsteps sounded in the hall. "How did you find out? Did mother call?"

"No." Kathy flipped on the kitchen light. "A man came by."

"A man!" Tina shrieked. "Would you like to explain?"

"A gentleman from Dudley, Smith and York came by to tell me I'm about to be a very wealthy lady."

"Give me a break." Tina rolled her eyes and poured herself a glass of white wine. "Aunt Catherine left *you* some money?"

"So it would seem."

Tina's eyebrows shot up. "How much?"

"I don't know." Kathy stooped down and pulled out the

aluminum spaghetti pot. "It can't be much Remember that old car she drove?" She looked at her sister as she filled the pot with water. "It was at least ten years old. Anyway, I have to call Monday and make an appointment with her attorney."

LATE MONDAY MORNING found Kathy rubbing the back of her neck. She'd arrived early to try to catch up on her work. As an illustrator for a card company, Kathy spent many hours bent over a drawing board. She took another sip of hot coffee, then stared down at the half-finished Christmas scene. It was hard to think of snow when the morning had been sultry and hot. And the bus trip without air conditioning hadn't helped. Then there was the other reason she had a hard time concentrating . . . She looked at the small business card for the dozenth time. Why did she keep putting off making the call? Most people would have been on the attorney's doorstep bright and early, demanding to know what they had inherited. But the old saying, "If it sounds too good to be true -- it probably is," kept whirling around her head.

Sighing, she dropped her pen and picked up the receiver, then dialed the number. Listening for the ring, Kathy glanced at her arms and found they had broken out in gooseflesh. Somehow, she had a feeling this very simple phone call was going to change her life. But for the good or bad, that was the big question?

"Good morning. Dudley, Smith and York. May I help you?" The female voice sounded business-like, efficient and rang out clear.

"Hi, I need to make an appointment with Mr. York."

"One moment. Let me get my book." There was silence and Kathy could hear the woman fumbling. "I've got it. What time would be convenient for you?"

"I would prefer late afternoon."

"Let me see . . ." The sound of pages flipping seemed to go on forever. "I'm afraid August is the earliest he can see you."

"August!" Kathy repeated. This Mr. York must be a very good lawyer. And if he was so much in demand why couldn't he drop her a nice little note and save her a lot of trouble?

"How about August twenty-fourth at one o'clock?"

Gosh, she had hoped it would have been sooner, but if that were the best. . . "That's fine. My name is Katherine Taylor."

"Miss Taylor! Why didn't you say so? Mr. York left instructions this morning that if you called he wanted to speak to you right away."

"Really?" Kathy was surprised by that bit of news.

"Just a minute. I'll buzz."

The phone rang twice. "Good morning, Katherine." The deep male voice carried an intriguing English accent. "I'm so glad you've called."

"The gentleman yesterday said it was important," Kathy's voice squeaked compared to the smooth accent on the other end. She cleared her throat and tried to sound professional. "I'm sorry, I'm bothering you, Mr. York. I know you must be busy, and your secretary did set up an appointment for me in August. I hope that's all right?"

"No. I'm afraid it isn't."

"Oh?"

"I'd like to see you right away. How about this afternoon at four o'clock?"

"Four? I--I can't." He sounded anxious to see her or was that her imagination? "I--I don't have a car; mine died last week." She laughed nervously. "Perhaps I can call my sister and see if she will take me."

"Good. Your aunt always talked a great deal about you. As a matter of fact, I feel I already know you, Katherine."

The way he enunciated each syllable of her name made chills run up her arms. "Are you serious?"

"Quite right. She had a special place in her heart for her niece and wanted to see you do better for yourself. My next appointment is here so I'll run for now. See you at four, goodbye."

"Bye." Her voice faded. She couldn't believe Aunt Catherine had spoken often about her. Kathy had tried to avoid the woman as much as possible because her aunt was so darn prim and proper.

She dialed her sister's number. It was a pain not having a car to drive. But since the small accident had been Kathy's fault, and she was broke, her feet would have to do for now.

"Hello, Tina speaking."

"Tina. Can you leave work a little early and take me by the lawyer's?"

"I had other plans. . ." There was silence. "But I'll switch them if you think it's *that* important. I sure will be glad when you get another car," she grumbled.

"Me too." Kathy placed the receiver in the cradle. Why couldn't she have a sweet, loving sister like everyone else instead of a beautiful, bossy sister who never did anything wrong and who'd had the knack for making Kathy feel inferior all her life?

As she picked up the paintbrush and glanced down at

her forgotten work, she mumbled, "Maybe I'll get enough money to at least buy a used car."

TINA GOT out and shut the car door. "I'm not going to sit out in the car and wait for you. I'm coming, too," Tina said as she caught up with Kathy. They entered the tall office building in New Orleans. "After all she was my aunt, too. I'm sure Aunt Catherine has left me something."

"I still can't believe she left me anything. Funny, I never thought of Aunt Catherine as having a lot of money, so I'm sure it's not much." Kathy looked at her sister's red suit. Tina appeared crisp and cool and didn't seem to notice the humid weather at all.

But Kathy's once-curly hair now hung straight and limp, and her dress didn't have the crisp lines her sister's. She had chosen a navy-blue tent dress because it was cooler and one of her more flattering garments. The white peter pan collar flattered her tan and made her gold eyes appear large.

Upon entering the office suite, Kathy automatically drew in her breath. The mahogany furniture and blue leather wing back chairs glistened. The decor was impressive to say the least.

"I'm Miss Taylor. I have an appointment with Mr. York."

The perfectly-dressed receptionist scanned the page, smiled brightly and motioned for them to take a seat.

Before Kathy sat down, she noticed a large painting over the couch. Her eyes searched the right-hand corner and sure enough the print was signed and numbered. There was definitely nothing shabby about this office.

Evidently, Mr. York was very successful. He'd probably been in business for many years.

"Mr. York will see you now."

Kathy and Tina followed the woman down the long hall to a set of double doors. The receptionist turned the brass knob then stood aside and allowed them to enter. The man sitting behind a Chippendale desk rose as they came in. Kathy's gaze darted to the tall impeccably dressed gentleman in a black, pinstriped suit. His tan spoke for his love of outdoors, and his coal black hair was combed to the side and begged to be touched. But the final straw, and Kathy's undoing was, his dark brown eyes. He was the spitting image of Pierce Brosnan, or as she called him, Remington Steele.

Much to Kathy's embarrassment, she had halted the moment he stood while Tina had properly taken her seat. Now Kathy found herself standing in the middle of the floor, staring at the best-looking man she'd ever laid eyes on. If only she were thin and beautiful like Tina. Hearing her sister clear her throat snapped Kathy out of her stupor.

Mr. York extended his hand, and she managed to walk over and place her fingers in his. His warm skin felt like a caress. She just wanted to die, or say, *Take me, I'm yours.*

"It's a pleasure to meet you, Miss Taylor."

Oh, God . . . that voice. His British accent was wonderful, crisp and clear. "Thank you." Kathy took her seat and wondered if he'd mind if she just sat back and stared at him for the rest of the day. "This is my sister, Tina."

"Tina." He nodded politely, but turned his attention right back to Kathy. "I'm sorry I have to meet you under these circumstances. Your aunt Catherine was not only a client, but a good friend." He opened a large brown envelope and pulled out an official looking document. "Shall we begin?"

Devon looked directly at Kathy. She noticed that his eyes held a warmth in them that made her smile, and the way his hair barely touched his starched white collar made her tremble. Now she wished she'd never seen a chocolate cake. "Please do."

> *"I, Catherine Dubois, being of sound mind and body, do bequeath my entire estate to my lovely niece, Katherine Taylor, and to the beautiful woman she will one day become."*

Devon looked up and smiled.

Kathy's face grew hot. She wondered if Mr. York wanted to laugh at that statement. Thank goodness, he didn't, but continued to read.

> *"However, my will is not without conditions. My niece needs to prove to me that she is capable of handling such a sum of money."*

Kathy shifted in her chair. She knew it was too good to be true. For a couple of thousand dollars, Aunt Catherine probably wanted the world.

"How much money?" Tina couldn't keep quiet any longer.

"If you'll let me finish," Devon politely responded.

> *"Until such time as Kathy meets these requirements all money spent must be approved by my administrator, Devon York, someone I have*

admired over the years and trust to have my last
wishes carried out.
"There will be a charity ball held on December 24,
of this year. Providing that Kathy has met the
qualifications, the bulk of one million dollars
will be hers at that time."

"A million dollars!" Kathy jumped straight out of her chair.

"Yes, Miss Taylor. You will be a wealthy lady one day."

"A million dollars," Kathy repeated, feeling a little dizzy by all the blood that had rushed from her head.

"What about me?" Tina asked. "After all I'm her niece, too."

"Let me see," Devon scanned the page. "I'm sorry you are not mentioned, Tina. He turned his attention back to the will. If Kathy fails, Catherine's wealth will go to charity."

"But that's not fair!"

"That may be true, Tina, but your aunt evidently saw things differently."

"Let me get this straight." Kathy sank back down in her chair. "My aunt left me a million dollars?" She contemplated the notion, then looked him square in the eye. Where in the world did the woman get so much money? She hadn't lived like a wealthy woman. "Are you sure, Mr. York?"

A deep, rich laughter rumbled from his chest. "Yes, I'm positive. And please call me Devon since we will be getting to know each other over the next few months." She saw his gaze had fixed on her lips, and when his brown eyes lifted to hers there was something unreadable in their depths.

"So I can spend money as long as I consult with you first?"

"That's correct."

"You mentioned some conditions."

"Yes, there is one stipulation. Excuse me." He picked up the receiver and punched a couple of numbers, "Please bring me the dress."

Dress? Kathy frowned. What did a dress have to do with anything? And why did he want it in the middle of their business meeting? She heard the door open behind them. The receptionist entered carrying a garment bag and handed it to Devon.

"Mr. York--Devon," Kathy corrected herself. "Do you mind putting your personal life aside for a moment. I believe we were discussing my aunt's will."

"That we were, Katherine. But I needed this . . ." He indicated the bag as he laid it on the table. "Before I could continue."

"A dress? I don't understand."

"Why not a gown," Tina snapped. "She's left you everything else."

Kathy wanted to hear what the man had to say not Tina's whining. "Shut up, Tina. It's not my fault Aunt Catherine left me something." Kathy turned back to Devon. "My aunt has left me a gown?"

"In a way. Let me explain." He began to read again.

> *"My niece must meet the following requirement before claiming her inheritance. She must show me that she is capable of taking charge of her life. On December twenty-fourth, Katherine must wear this black gown to present the Dubois award."*

"That's all?" Kathy couldn't believe that was the only stipulation. It was much too easy. Then she noticed Devon had started unzipping the clothing bag. He then pulled out a slim, sexy silhouette dress of black crepe. The top was embellished in sequins and the straight skirt had a split up to the knee. There was only one big problem. . . "Don't you think that dress is a little small?"

"I believe this gown is a size eight," Devon told her.

"Just like I said, it's too small." She saw a glint of humor in his eyes. "It must have been my aunt's dress."

"No." He shook his head before patiently saying. "This outfit was designed especially for you."

"Well, the seamstress had to have been drunk!"

Devon laughed. "You must wear *this* dress to inherit your aunt's wealth."

"Are you crazy or just a little blind?" She flung her hand at the gown. "I'm a size . . ." She'd been about to say size *sixteen,* but nothing--not even a million dollars--would make her admit that and especially to someone as gorgeous as Mr. York. "Anyway, I can't wear that thing!"

"I've had others accuse me of being crazy, but I assure you, I'm not blind." His smile came so naturally that it drew her attention to his strong jaw and masculine chin. There was such confidence about him -- something she, herself, had lacked over the last few years. He poured a glass of water from the pitcher on his desk took a sip then continued. "I believe the idea your aunt had in mind was for you to lose weight."

Tina started to laugh. "That means Kathy would have to lose four dress sizes." Holding a hand over her mouth to conceal her mirth, Tina looked at her sister. "Kathy, you might as well kiss that money goodbye."

Kathy came out of her stupor and glared at her sister.

"I would have only six months to shed that weight. I can't do that."

"You mean you'd throw up your hands and quit without making an effort?" Devon stared at Kathy as if he knew what she was thinking. "That's a lot of money to give up without trying."

"But, I can't do it."

"You sure can't," Tina agreed.

"How do you know without giving it a go?" Devon argued in typical lawyer style. "After all, what's the worst that could happen?"

"Kathy doesn't have any willpower," Tina informed him. "So you're wasting your time, Mr. York."

Tina's lack of faith pushed a button in Kathy. She glanced sideways at her sister who had never had any faith in her, but what if she did lose weight? She would never again have to worry about money again. And never have to depend on her sister when things went wrong which they usually did. Devon was right. She had nothing to lose and everything to gain.

"I'll do it," Kathy muttered, determined to show Tina and wipe that smug smile off her face.

"You mean, you're going on a diet?" Tina asked, astonished. "Think of how many diets you've tried . . . and with little success, I might add."

"That might be true, Tina, but I'm going to give it my best."

"Good!" That was what Devon wanted to hear. There was a spunkiness about Katherine that he found fresh and appealing. She was different. Like a rare gem. "Is there anything you need at the moment."

"A car would be nice."

Devon remembered Katherine had said her car had

died, which he presumed meant wrecked. And he really couldn't blame Kathy for not wanting to rely on her sister. "I agree." He looked at his calendar. "I'm busy the rest of the week; however, I'm free Saturday. I could pick you up Saturday morning, and we can look for a car and have a bite of lunch. How does that sound?"

"I don't want to bother you."

"It's no problem, Katherine. Remember, we're partners now."

Kathy stared into the dark brown eyes across the desk, and shivered at the blatant sensuality that radiated from him.

He was her partner?

Now that was a proposition she found *very* appealing!

CHAPTER 2

*D*evon stared at the closed door.

What a young lady! He couldn't remember when he'd enjoyed a meeting so much. But now he wondered just what was he getting himself into? Sliding the legal documents back into the brown envelope, he leaned back in his leather chair and thought of Catherine Dubois and the special friendship they had shared.

Catherine had been wise beyond her years and had brought him down a notch or two when he was a young ambitious lawyer. Devon had thought of her as his friend and confidant, and she had spoken often of her niece and the hopes she had for Katherine. Mrs. Dubois had called her niece a diamond in the rough. And now that he'd met her, Devon found he also agreed.

As a matter of fact, he felt like he'd known Katherine for years. She would probably blush if she knew all the things her aunt had told him about her. He remembered the many pictures Mrs. Dubois had kept of her niece. They were all around the house, but his favorite sat upon the piano.

Kathy had been thin in that picture with eyes of shimmering gold. He hated to admit it but that picture had stirred his desire more than once.

When she entered his office today, Devon had been surprised at the weight she'd gained. Her aunt had told him that Kathy was an emotional eater with very little willpower when it came to food.

Devon knew the feeling all to well. Back in England, he'd been heavy, as his father had pointed out on several occasions. And he'd been more or less an outcast among the youth, the last one chosen to play ball. But all that changed when he entered college and began seriously playing sports -- exercise and eating right became his burning goal.

Now, if he could only teach Katherine a little of his self-discipline. Smiling, he could still picture Katherine coming to her feet when he'd told her a million dollars. Her eyes had sparkled like twenty-four karat gold. Even though she was over weight, her face was beautiful with striking features. He sensed a beautiful woman lurking just beneath the surface.

However, finding that woman could be a little more difficult than he'd first thought. He had expected to meet a meek woman thankful to inherit a fortune. Not a strong-willed young lady who wanted no part of the deal and the strings that came with it.

Perhaps he'd been too hasty to make this agreement. He had nothing in common with the girl. After all, he did have a heavy caseload and needed no further aggravation. But Catherine had been too persuasive. She wanted him to get involved with her niece so he could help the girl.

"Well Catherine, I've kept my promise."

"Wasn't he the best-looking thing you've ever laid eyes on?" Tina gushed after they left the office.

"He was rather nice looking," Kathy commented nonchalantly, though nonchalant was not how she felt. Devon was very good looking, but he wouldn't have glanced twice at her if it wasn't his job. She knew that. However, she had to admit, he had been pleasant, and she could never tire of looking at those dreamy eyes of his. "Did you see *that* dress?"

"I sure did. You've got your work cut out for you if you ever expect to get into that slinky thing." Tina unlocked the car doors, and they slipped into the vehicle.

"I guess it will be salads for a while." Kathy shook her head as she dreaded the thought.

"Lots of salads." Tina laughed. "I'll give you a month at the most before you've ditched your diet."

Kathy looked at her ever-doubting sister. Wouldn't it be wonderful if, for once, she succeeded in something? She grinned. Perhaps she could make Tina eat her words.

That would be worth more than the money.

After Aunt Catherine's funeral, the rest of the week seemed to drag by as Kathy alternated between salads and cottage cheese. Of course, she rewarded herself every now and then with some malted milk balls. But they were small packs, she reasoned. Now she was down to the last bag which she had stuffed in the corner of her purse just in case she needed a sugar fix . . . you know . . . dire emergency.

She found herself looking forward to Saturday . . . not because she would be spending the day with Devon, but the fact she'd be getting a new car, or at least that's what she kept telling herself.

Saturday morning found Kathy spending extra time in front of the mirror as she applied her makeup. She chose a lemon-yellow pantsuit with a tiny white stripe running through the material. She tied her hair back with white and yellow ribbons and added just a touch of rust-colored blush to her cheekbones.

Promptly at nine, Devon arrived dressed in white slacks and a chambray-blue shirt. He would turn any woman's head as he entered the front door . . . especially hers. "Ready, Luv?"

Luv? Kathy gave him a sidelong glance as she picked up her purse. Somehow, she wished she were the love of his life. She could well imagine those firm lips pressed against hers, and his strong arms wrapped protectively around her. The mere thought made her knees almost buckle. Just how long had it been since she'd kissed a man?

Too long. Kathy straightened and walked toward Devon, taking in the fragrance of his British Sterling. *God, help me not make a complete fool out of myself today*, she prayed.

"You look nice," Devon commented as they walked down the sidewalk.

"Thank you." She brushed off his compliment. "You're being kind."

"Kind?" He placed a hand on her shoulder before opening the door. "Kathy, one thing you should know. I don't say things I don't mean. As a matter of fact, some have accused me of having a sharp tongue. I repeat, you look very nice today. Yellow becomes you."

"Thank you," she murmured as she ducked into a dark

green jaguar. She appreciated the compliment, but why couldn't he have said beautiful, lovely, or cute? She knew why . . . nice was reserved for fat people. Kathy watched as Devon lowered his six-foot two frame into the driver's side.

"Have you had breakfast?"

"Unfortunately." She gave a scornful laugh. "I had a boiled egg." She held her nose in jest, producing immediate laughter from Devon, a sound she found all too thrilling. And to her surprise, she found she liked making him laugh. Something told her it wasn't something he did very often.

"Good girl," he praised her, then shifted the car into drive and pulled away from the curve.

She was glad Tina had been asleep so they could get an early start. Tina would have commanded Devon's attention the minute he walked through the door, and since she was beautiful and Kathy was plain Jane, there would have been no contest in where Devon's attentions lay.

Kathy cleared her throat. "Are you in a big hurry this morning?

Devon gave her a sideways glance, wondering what she had on her mind. Perhaps, she thought he was driving too fast. He could tell by the way she held her hands that she'd been hesitant to ask the question. "No. Why do you ask?"

"If you don't mind -- and I understand completely if you do mind -- could you stop at the corner store up there." She pointed ahead, adding, "So I can get a loaf of bread?"

"I thought you had eaten breakfast."

"Not for me . . ." Kathy laughed, and Devon found he liked the sound of her lyrical voice and laughter. When Kathy smiled, she had a radiant glow about her, and he was finding out minute by minute how endearing this young woman could be.". . . It's for the ducks."

Devon made a sweeping turn into the store parking lot before looking at her. "Would you care to explain?"

"On Saturday mornings, I normally go to Angier Lake to feed the ducks. And I thought, if you didn't mind, we could run by and feed them this morning."

"I haven't fed ducks since I was a lad," he told Kathy.

After purchasing a loaf of bread, they drove the three miles to the lake. They got out of the car and walked to the water's edge.

Devon looked around, oblivious to his beautiful surrounds. "I don't see anything but water."

"Are you always such a pessimist?" Kathy asked as she undid the twist-tie on the loaf of bread.

"I'm just merely stating facts. I don't see any feathered fowl."

"Well, as an attorney, you should be aware that sometimes the facts are hidden." Grabbing a few slices of bread, she handed them to Devon. "Crumble the bread and you'll soon see the ducks."

He rolled his eyes but followed Kathy's lead, tearing the bread into little pieces. Sure enough, when he looked up again, there were ten to twelve ducks swimming across the lake. "Here they come."

"I see."

He watched as they swam to shore. "I think the mallards are my favorite."

"They're mine, too. See that one." She pointed. "He looks like he has a top hat on his head."

Devon chuckled. "Is he supposed to look like that?"

"I'm not sure." Kathy shrugged. "Look! The gray mallard has babies," her voice lifted in excitement as she bent and tossed tiny shreds to the balls of fuzz scrambling upon shore.

He watched the six little ducks waddling behind their mother while the sound of Kathy's gay laughter floated in the air. Devon glanced at the blue water and saw how the ripples glinted in the sun. Everything was surrounded by olive-green grass, and on the other side of the lake, white and yellow wildflowers dotted the landscape.

When had he last taken time to notice the lovely things around him? He sighed. It was amazing how life could shut you in until one became a functioning robot.

What amazed Devon the most was the jovial young woman in front of him. She seemed to make the whole scene come alive. At this very moment, he felt relaxed more than he had in a long time.

"Isn't it nice here? Look over there. We have a pair of swans." Her eyes brightened before she continued. "They haven't been here before. They're so graceful and a lot prettier than the ducks. I would like to be just like them." She sighed.

"You do know that they are quite ugly when they're young?"

"Are you calling me an ugly duckling?"

Devon laughed. "Not exactly. I'm just saying one should never judge a book by its cover." He stared at her, picturing the beauty hidden within her. This attraction of his wasn't in the job description, he warned himself.

"Did you know that swans mate for life?"

"What a novel idea in this day and time," he said a little more sarcastically than he meant to.

"So you don't believe in love, Devon?" Kathy's tone shifted from the bubbly one she had a moment ago.

As he stared at her, the wind blew a stray hair across

her face and, without thinking, he reached up and brushed the strand away from her face. Then he smiled at her. God, her skin was smooth. "I do believe in love; though, I'm not sure I've ever found it." He cleared his throat. "What do you want out of life?"

Kathy needed for her own self-protection, to break this sudden intimacy she felt. She leaned her head to the side, she teased, "Is this an essay question?"

"Not hardly, Luv."

"In that case, I'd like what most people long for: a home, a loving family, and children." She gave him a wry smile. "But so far that seems like an unreachable dream or at least with the men I've known."

Without warning, Devon reached out and took her hand. "Perhaps your luck is changing."

What was that supposed to mean? Kathy stared at him with wide eyes. Was he going to be some magical fairy godfather that stepped into her life and made it better? Somehow she doubted that.

No one could work miracles. But while she had him, she was definitely going to enjoy the view.

He gave a tug on her hand and said, "Come on." When the last few crumbs disappeared, they made their way back to the car. Both remained quiet for a few miles.

As Kathy stared out the window, she remembered their original mission. She looked forward to having her own car again, so she wouldn't be so dependent on her sister. "Where are we going? I saw an advertisement for Slick Sam's Auto Sales. I'm sure we could purchase a good used car."

Devon looked amused. "Come on, Katherine, you can't be serious. Slick Sam's? Give me a break. I do believe I can do better by you."

"You can call me Kathy."

"I suppose I could." He smiled as he glanced at her. "But Katherine is such a lovely name, however, I shall call you Kathy." And Devon did find loveliness about this woman. True she was overweight, but her unusual golden eyes held a spark within their depths that he found intriguing. He wondered just what made her tick? Somehow, he had the feeling he wouldn't be bored finding the answer. He was also surprised he had been looking forward to today. Usually he wouldn't be caught dead shopping with a woman. So why had he jumped and offered to help her? The only answer could be . . . out of loyalty to her aunt. Of course . . . that was it.

He whipped the car into the Oldsmobile dealership. "Let's start here."

There were at least fifty cars on the lot, Kathy thought as she wandered over to a used Datsun and took a seat. "How about this one?" She glanced up at Devon as he neared the car.

"It will not do." His crisp upper class English accent was evident.

"Why?"

"For starters, it's used." He stood with his arms folded, a sure indication she should take his word and not question him. "I want you to have a new car. And the second reason is it's too small."

"But, I fit in here just fine."

"I can see that, but once you get your friends in the car it will be crowded. Besides when you get married, unless you marry a small man, your husband will never be comfortable." Devon thought about what he'd just said.

Of course, Kathy would marry, but somehow the thought bothered him. He had found himself thinking about her more than once this past week, and he wondered why a simple meeting with a girl he'd just met had lingered in his mind. It wasn't as if he were a monk. He had dated dozens of girls. Or should he say dozens of boring women whom he never gave a second thought to? To say the least, when this young woman who now sat frowning at him from the car stayed on his mind, he had to ask the question why. Unfortunately, he had found no answer to his question . . . at least not yet.

"Gee, I didn't know I was contemplating marriage." Kathy laughed, wondering what in the world ever made him think of such a thing. "My husband could always run along behind the car like a dutiful spouse."

Devon chuckled, then opened the car door for her. "And no doubt you'd suggest just that."

They looked at black cars, red cars, and blue cars. Some were big, some small. Kathy would have taken the first one she came upon -- anything beat walking -- but Devon again said it wasn't good enough. Evidently the man was used to the very best life had to offer.

Finally, they spotted a white Cutlass Supreme with blue leather interior. "Oh, Devon, this is perfect." She clutched his arm, and her eyes glistened with excitement.

"Do you have your heart set on this one, Luv?"

She nodded, and he saw the exuberance of a child. His heart gave a little twist as he smiled at her. In many ways, Kathy seemed just that . . . untouched and unspoiled. And something about her made him feel good, young and alive.

"I agree. You've made a good choice." He acknowledged before the attorney in him took over and began questioning the salesman and negotiating the price.

Kathy positioned herself behind the steering wheel of her new car and started the motor. She looked up at Devon who stood by the door. "Thank you for helping me with my selection." Kathy almost wished they hadn't found the car this soon so she could spend more time with this handsome, fascinating man. But she could think of no way to prolong their meeting.

"You're welcome, Luv."

She stared at him a moment longer before reluctantly saying, "Goodbye."

"Not so fast." He reached in the window and placed his hand on her arm.

Kathy felt a dizzy rush of adrenaline, which caused her to draw in her breath. If the mere touch of his hand left her hot, bothered, and feeling like this, she'd be mere putty in his hands if he ever made a real advance.

"I believe I promised to buy lunch. Why don't you follow me?" he suggested. "I've a reservation at the Country Club."

Kathy smiled and managed not to shout, *Oh boy, lunch!*

AT THE COUNTRY CLUB, they sat on a beautiful white veranda overlooking several tennis courts. A ceiling fan turned lazily above their heads as Kathy quietly appraised the women sitting at the other tables. They appeared perfectly polished, and every hair was in place.

Kathy leaned over the table and whispered to Devon. "Are you sure I'm dressed properly?" She felt totally intimidated by the posh, *slim* women sitting around the tables. They all smiled at Devon -- no doubt he knew them all personally.

"Of course, you are." He brushed off her concern. "What would you like for lunch?"

Kathy held up a large menu. Everything looked and sounded delicious. There were a variety of things to choose from: steaks, spaghetti and fettuccini, but she should probably stick with something light. "Let's see. How about a hamburger steak and some French fries?"

Devon's eyes widened in disbelief. "Isn't that a little fattening?"

"I was going to order the hamburger without the bun," she defended, wondering what he would have said if she'd ordered the spaghetti and meatballs. Oh, God, she'd kill for that.

"How about some tuna salad on lettuce?" Devon suggested.

"And a side order of French fries?"

"No, Kathy. You're dieting."

Her dark eyebrows slanted in a frown, then she conceded. "Gosh, you know how to win a girl's heart. Tuna! Now, why didn't I think of such a nutritious feast?"

Devon chuckled. "I tell you what. I'll have the same thing, so you will not feel you're suffering."

She liked that idea and smiled. Looking to her left, Kathy saw the tennis courts starting to fill up. "This is a beautiful place. Do you come here often?"

"I try to play tennis once or twice a week. And they do have their own exercise rooms, so I get a good workout. Have you started an exercise program?" He had to hide his smile at her astonishment.

"Was I supposed to?"

"It will help achieve your goal faster, but we're getting ready to fix that problem."

"We?"

"That's right. I have decided it will be better if I take an active hand in your weight loss so you don't slip off your

38

diet." Devon paused for a moment in surprise. He couldn't believe he'd just said that. What was it about this lady that made him do strange things? True, he wanted her to meet her goal. But he was busy. He had two major cases he needed to work on, yet he'd just volunteered to be a training coach for an overweight girl he'd just met.

"I can touch my toes at home, and it won't cost me anything." That was a joke, Kathy thought. She couldn't remember the last time she'd been able to see her toes -- much less touch them.

"There is no need to worry about money. It will come out of your estate, and you're going to be doing more than touching your toes."

Their conversation came to an abrupt halt when lunch arrived. Kathy munched on tuna and carrot sticks and thought about what Devon had just offered. There could be benefits to this exercise thing, she thought as she sipped her tea and looked at him from beneath her thick lashes. He chatted about some cases he was working on, which gave her time to stare at him. It seemed strange how Devon talked so freely with her. Usually two people who'd just met had to think hard of what to say, but Devon seemed so at ease with her . . . like he'd known her forever. Of course, it was probably her imagination. He was probably at ease with everyone.

Now back to this exercise thing, Kathy scolded herself. She just had to keep her mind off Devon's physical attributes. If she exercised, at least she'd be spending more time with him. A slow smile formed. Perhaps, she could stand a little torture.

"How come a hunk like you isn't married?" Kathy paused mouth open, wishing she could stuff the words back into her mouth. Damn! Why didn't she think before she spoke?

He chuckled and Kathy felt her cheeks heat with a blush. "I'm sorry. Let's pretend I didn't say anything. Actually, I'm at my best when I don't talk."

"So you'd like to get personal?" His eyes danced with something more than amusement. This was the second time the lady had brought up marriage. "Why would you think I should be married? Do I appear old?"

"N--no, it's not that. I--It's just . . ." God this was embarrassing because she could think of every reason he should be married. "You are good looking as, I'm sure, you already know. I just thought some woman would have snared you by now."

"Thank you for the compliment." He nodded his head. "But to be very honest, I've never met anyone I've wanted to spend the rest of my life with. How about yourself?" The question was so simply asked.

"Who would want me?"

Devon laid his fork down and frowned. "Why do you put yourself down? You're quite lovely."

"You meant *nice*."

"No." He gave her a disapproving look. "I meant lovely."

"Yeah, sure."

"It's true you are overweight, but it doesn't hide your beauty."

"You could have fooled me." Kathy gave a sarcastic laugh. "Why are you going out of your way for me? I know you were my aunt's solicitor, and you do have a job to do. But aren't you going beyond the call of duty?"

His dark eyes stared at her, yet he said nothing. Great! Kathy thought. Here was the man she would really like to know better . . . and now she had to challenge his intentions. Then again, maybe it was just as well. What chance did she have?

"You don't like my company?" His voice didn't hold the touch of anger she'd expected.

"That's not what I meant. I do like you but . . ."

He held up his hand to cut her off. Unexpectedly, Devon leaned across the table, and took her hand in his. "Kathy, I know this sounds strange, but I . . ."

CHAPTER 3

"I hate to tell ya, Kat, but I don't think that's an original design." Jack Walker's voice broke into Kathy's thoughts.

Kathy sat at her drawing table with her jaw propped on her left hand as she drew circles on her artist pad. Jack's voice pulled her out of the daze she'd been in for the last hour. Looking up, she smiled across the table to the man who had been her good friend and confidant for a long time. "I don't feel creative today."

"Well, don't tell the boss." Jack grinned. "Is it something you want to talk about? Or someone?"

"I'm that obvious?" Kathy felt herself blush as she crumpled up the piece of paper and threw it in the trash can.

"Kind of." Jack leaned back in his chair and put his hands behind his head. It's that faraway look in your eyes that gives you away. So tell me . . . What's his name?"

She frowned at Jack for knowing her so well. "Devon."

"And I suppose it's too late to tell you to be careful."

Jack lowered his chair. Picking up his pencil, he began tapping it against his drawing board.

She could tell he was prepared to lecture her since he considered himself her personal advisor. "Afraid so," she admitted.

"Does he feel the same?"

She shrugged her shoulders. "I don't know."

"Give it time, Kat. And don't go telling him how you feel. I have a hunch this time you've met a good guy." Jack gave a mischievous laugh. "'Cause you've already met all the bad ones . . . there can't be any left."

He cut his eyes behind her and slid a drawing in Kathy's direction. "Here comes Old Man Wood. Better look like you're doing something productive."

"Miss Taylor." Their boss cleared his voice. "I--I just had a very interesting call from a Mr. York requesting a week of vacation for you. I was under the impression you had taken all your vacation." He wrinkled his nose and peered over a pair of wire-framed reading glasses.

"That's true, Mr. Wood."

"Exactly, what I told Mr. York. We have deadlines here. I can't let people off without a good reason."

"But, Mr. Wood, I need --"

"I asked Mr. York just who he was," Mr. Wood cut her off, evidently not wanting to hear what she had to say on the subject. "I was under the expression you were single and could speak for yourself?

"Yes, I am."

"That's what I thought, but he informed me in no uncertain terms he was your attorney. Is that correct?"

"Yes. He was my aunt's attorney."

"Was?"

"She's dead." Kathy informed him.

"Well, I'm sorry," Old Man Wood apologized, but the look in his beady little eyes told her a different story. "I told your attorney that you couldn't have the time off. It's impossible at this time."

"I understand." Kathy really didn't see why Mr. Wood was going into this long drawn out conversation when all he really had to do was tell her no.

"Well, I'm glad you do." He gave a half-hearted chuckle. "Because Mr. York did not! He informed me you quit as of today, and I could draw up your severance pay."

"He did what!" Kathy jumped to her feet. "He had no right."

"As your attorney and financial adviser, he informed me he had every right." Mr. Wood held out an envelope. "Here's your pay. If you'll please sign this release form." He pointed. "You can be on your way."

Fuming inside, she scribbled her name. How could Devon destroy her income? She'd kill him.

"Good day." Old Man Wood turned on his heel but called back to her. "Please clean out your desk before you leave."

"Kat, I don't believe what just happened." Poor Jack's face had grown pale. "That's too bad."

"I don't believe it either." She jerked open the drawer and started cleaning out her desk. "You just wait till I see Mr. York!"

"This isn't by any chance the same man you were just sitting here day-dreaming about?"

"The very one." She cut her eyes up and dared him to laugh. "I must have been crazy."

"It sounds like Mr. Perfect is used to calling the shots. I hope he can support you."

"Oh, Devon is capable of that, I assure you. But he's

going to find out real fast he's not running my life." She slammed her paper into a box. "I am."

"Give him hell, Kat!" Jack came over and gave her a hug. "And keep in touch."

BARGING INTO DEVON'S OFFICE, Kathy attacked the first person that came into sight. "Tell Mr. York I want to see him now." She stared down at the receptionist.

"I don't believe you had an ap--"

Kathy pointed her finger at the girl, then realizing that the waiting room was full, lowered her voice. "Unless you want a real ugly scene out here, I suggest you tell Mr. York I want to see him now. Not by appointment . . . not later . . . but now!" The woman's eyes grew wide, and Kathy assumed she must look like a crazed person. Perhaps one that would draw out a gun at any moment and open fire on the entire office. This time the receptionist didn't argue.

"This way, Miss Taylor." Kathy was quickly shown down the hall. She entered Devon's office and slammed the door on the poor girl before whirling around to attack. "How dare you!"

"Now, Kathy." Devon stood up holding his hands out as if he was fending off a tiger. "I thought you might be a little upset . . ."

"A--A little upset. Is that what you call this?" She began to pace in front of his desk. "Well, let me tell you. I'm more than a little upset." She stopped and leaned across the desk. "I'm damn mad, and if I had a gun I'd probably shoot you. You're interfering with my livelihood, and you have absolutely no right!" She slammed her hands on the desk. "I'm not wealthy yet, and I don't have a husband to support me."

"I'll take care of you," Devon said calmly. He didn't look the least bit upset by her ravings. "And you'll be wealthy by December."

"Yeah sure. But there are a whole lot of 'if's' in there. What if I don't meet my goal, Devon? Have you ever thought about that?"

"You'll meet it," he said with confidence.

"What if I don't? Are you going to marry and support me?"

"Are you proposing?" A hint of laughter appeared in his eyes.

"No! And don't make light of this situation. I'm not a toy, Devon, for your amusement when you're bored. You have no right to make such decisions without consulting me first," she reprimanded. "Just who do you think you are?"

Devon pushed his chair back and stood. "A friend who thought he had your best interest at heart." He came around the desk to stand in front of her. "Listen, this is probably the best thing that could have happened. You don't need to be working for that old geezer. Besides, I've booked you into Weatherford next week. And you know bloody well you didn't like that job anyway."

Feeling her anger ebb away, she said in a quiet voice, "But it should have been my decision to quit, not yours."

"Point taken." His brown eyes darkened, and for just a moment he looked like a small child who had just been reprimanded. "I'm sorry, Luv. But I think you'll agree later, I did right by you."

"You're incorrigible." She still tried to hang onto her

anger, but when Devon smiled, those twin dimples became evident. He was simply irresistible.

"But lovable," he reminded her.

"I'll let you know later on that count," she retorted wryly. "I guess I better go. You have an office full of people." She turned and bumped his arm, sending her purse to the floor. When she bent down her protesting muscles caused her to groan.

"I see we're a little sore this afternoon."

"A little hell," she mumbled in her upside down position before straightening. "Try a whole lot."

Devon chuckled at Kathy's direct way of telling things. It was her freshness he liked best. "We'll work those kinks out tonight."

"I'm too sore." She shook her head in protest. "I can't exercise these weary bones."

"Of course you can. Besides we must get you in shape for Weatherford. If you think I'm tough, just wait until you get there."

"Great. It sounds like you're sending me to a boot camp. You sure do enjoy torturing me."

He put his arm around her and walked with her to the door. "Not really, Luv. But I must say, you have proven to be a real challenge. Now run along, and I'll see you tonight."

THE REST of the week went by in a haze of activity. Devon picked her up every night. They would have something light to eat then go the club to work out. By Friday, some of Kathy's soreness had begun to subside, thank goodness. Now she didn't moan and groan with every step.

Kathy felt as if she'd known Devon all her life, and if she hadn't fallen in love with him before, she'd definitely fallen now. The bubbly, happy feeling she experienced when she was with him was great. When she had stepped on the scales and had lost five pounds, she beamed under his praise.

SATURDAY MORNING FOUND Kathy packing her bags for Weatherford. Tina came in and sat on the bed to watch.

"What time are you leaving?" Tina asked.

"Devon is picking me up at 10:30." Kathy took a folded shirt and placed it in the suitcase. "My plane leaves at 12:00."

"Since he's taking you to the airport, can I drive your car while you're gone?"

Kathy reached in her purse for the car keys. "Sure." She handed them to her.

Tina picked up a silk, fuchsia blouse. "When did you get this?"

"Devon took me shopping. Said I needed some new clothes."

"I envy you, sis. You don't have to work, and you can go shopping whenever you want. And now you seem to have a good-looking man following you around for whatever the reason."

Kathy stopped packing and looked at Tina. "What do you mean by that remark?"

Tina shrugged her shoulders. "I don't like the way he controls your life. First, he has you fired, and now he's sending you off to some swanky resort. I sure hope Devon has your best interest at heart."

Kathy stared at her sister. Devon had accused Tina of the same thing. "I think he has my welfare at heart. He's a good friend, that's all."

"Somehow, sister dear, I think it's more than friends for you." Tina raised her eyebrow and gave her that all-knowing look. "But what happens after you've met your goal?"

Kathy shrugged her shoulders. "I've not given it much thought."

"Well, you should. You'll be a wealthy heiress. Men will be after you, and you'll never know if it's you they love or your money."

"I'm not wealthy now, and it doesn't seem to matter to Devon," Kathy countered. "Besides, he doesn't need the money."

"Are you sure? Everybody needs money. Even if they have money they want more."

"Stop it!" Kathy said a little louder than she meant to. "I don't know why you don't like Devon, but I won't stand here and listen to you putting him down."

"I only want what's best for you."

Kathy shut her suitcase and snapped the latches. "I hate to tell you big sister, but I'm old enough to take care of myself."

The doorbell chimed, and Tina slid off the bed. "I hope you're right, sister dear, I hope you're right."

DEVON FLIPPED on the left turn signal and turned into New Orleans International Airport.

Kathy had been listening halfhearted to him talk about

a case that was proving difficult when she simply asked, "Are you rich?"

Devon looked at her while putting his foot on the brake at the parking gate. "I can tell you were very interested in my case," he joked before taking the ticket from the machine. The gate swung up and they started to move again. "What kind of question was that?"

Kathy really felt embarrassed she had asked at all, but she had and couldn't back down now. "I thought it was a simple question." She played it off as something she might ask anyone. Devon swung into the parking place. "You drive an expensive car, and you seem to have a good business. You probably even live in a big house." She shrugged her shoulders. "I was just curious, that's all."

"I see." He turned in the seat and stared at her. "I don't suppose I'd say I was wealthy, but I do live comfortably. Does that satisfy your curiosity?"

Kathy nodded. "I know you think I'm crazy, but you seem to know so much about me, and I know very little about you."

Devon stared a moment before speaking, "I believe you're right, Luv, so we'll fix that problem." He leaned toward her. "Upon your return, I'll tell you all my deep, dark secrets," he whispered.

Kathy smiled. "If I return. I could be dead by the end of the week."

"Then you'll never know all my secrets," he replied as he opened the car door.

Once in the airport, Devon checked Kathy's bags and walked her to the check-in counter where everyone had just begun to line up at the gate.

"What are you going to do while I'm away?" Kathy

asked. Then she added, "I bet you're going to pig out while I'm starving in prison."

Devon chuckled and held up his right hand, placing the other over his heart. "I promise, I'll eat rabbit food while you're gone. And if you had been listening to me in the car instead of worrying about my financial status, you would have known I'll probably be working late every night on the McLeod case."

Kathy reached up and touched his smooth cheek. "Poor baby."

"Final Boarding." The call echoed above their heads.

"I guess that's me." She slung her purse over her arm.

Devon smiled down at her. "Be a good girl and don't give those poor women a hard time."

Kathy's gold eyes studied him with curious intensity. There was a hint of mischief in their depths. "I'll try." She tilted her head to the side and her brown hair swung about her face. "Are you going to miss me, Devon?"

"Yes, Luv. I believe I am." He bent down and kissed her ever so lightly. "Now run along before you miss your plane."

"See you in a week."

"Bye." Devon waved as he watched her turn to go. "Kathy," he called right before she entered the boarding hall. She looked back at him. For a moment, he couldn't say anything. Finally, he said, "I do care."

He saw her warm smile, and it was all Devon could do not to go after her. She seemed to be a fever in his blood. He was used to being in control in any situation and always had been. But when he was with Kathy all his circuits seemed to get crossed up, and he was liable to do or say anything. Maybe it would be good to have this week away from her.

"Excuse me, sir. Are you boarding?" the woman at the gate asked.

Devon realized he still stood staring at the doorway. "No, I'm not," he mumbled before he turned and walked away. If he was glad to have this time away from Kathy.

Why did he feel so empty inside?

CHAPTER 4

*K*athy stared out the plane window at the white billowing clouds. She was on her way to the fat farm. Devon had said she would come back a new woman; now she sat wondering if that would be true.

Staring at a fluffy white cloud, she tried to make sense of her churning emotions. Could she be lucky enough to have someone like Devon fall in love with her? Kathy sensed he felt something, but would he miss her while she was gone? Then she thought of Whitney. No, he probably wouldn't miss her at all.

Shutting her eyes, Kathy pictured his face with that dark complexion and smoothly shaven jaw. But it was his expression when she had turned to look back at him that made her pulse quicken. She could still hear his words. "I do care." It might not be much, but it was a start. She knew there was some kind of bond between them and warning bells sounded in her head. Her thoughts went scurrying back to her old love, Bill. She had tried to be perfect for him, laughing in all the right places, wearing all the right clothes. But evidently, she'd failed miserably because he'd married the nurse in his office -- who was pregnant with his child.

Needless to say, nobody had to dump water over her head to let her know Bill hadn't been faithful. He went back to the woman he'd been dating before her.

Now she was heading in the same direction again. If Devon did fall in love with her, would it be only a short time before he went back to Whitney? Having protected her emotions for so long, a part of her didn't want to feel anything for Devon. Should she risk taking a chance? That was a question she couldn't answer . . . at least not now . . . perhaps later.

A LIMO WAITED at the front of the Yuma Airport. The chauffeur gathered her luggage, then opened the door politely for her. Kathy felt important as heads turned and watched when she entered the car.

She had to laugh when she heard one woman whisper to another, "Who was that?"

Kathy had to resist the urge to roll down the window and yell, "Nobody -- Nobody at all." Staring out the window, Kathy rode in silence. She thought about engaging the chauffeur in conversation, but she wasn't sure it was proper, and she didn't want to appear like a hick, so she remained quiet. Glancing down at her hand, Kathy saw that it trembled, and she had to admit she was a little afraid. She had only traveled once before but never alone. Now here she was in the middle of nowhere and she didn't know anyone.

Looking out the window, she noticed everything had changed since they left the sprawling town of Yuma. The land was brown and barren and, at the moment, didn't look very hospitable. So far there wasn't a whole lot she liked about Arizona. Kathy was just about to tell the driver to turn around when the car slowed down. Oh, God, it was the gate to hell.

Displayed across the entrance in bold black letters was the name WEATHERFORD. The car made a left turn and they entered what appeared to be paradise. This place was unbelievable. The lush green shrubs and perfectly manicured lawns looked like a picture cut out of a magazine and pasted in the middle of the desert. As they neared the main clubhouse, Kathy noticed that the porches were flanked by trellises full of climbing vines.

The driver showed Kathy into an office where she had only to wait for a minute before a woman dressed in a beige summer suit appeared.

"Welcome to Weatherford, Miss Taylor." The manager extended her hand. The smile somehow didn't reach her eyes, and Kathy sensed that the woman recognized the difference between them. Kathy knew she wasn't blue-blood material. "I'm Mrs. Engles and I hope you will enjoy your little visit with us, dear."

"I'm sure I will." Kathy watched the other woman and was surprised Mrs. Engles carried neither a whip nor a gun.

"Let me show you to your room so that you may settle in." She motioned for Kathy to follow her. "Mr. York said you're to have the best," the manager said as she held the door open.

As they moved along the veranda, Kathy noticed several women walking about the lawns and a few in an olympic-size pool. Everyone was dressed in fine clothing, but something wasn't right.

She turned to speak to Mrs. Engles. "Where are the fat people."

A look of horror crossed the manager's face, and Kathy felt like she had truly insulted the woman, perhaps she should have said large.

Mrs. Engles batted her eyes. "I--I beg your pardon?"

"I said, where are the fat people? The women I see here look great. I don't see that they need any help at all. Perhaps one or two might be considered chubby, but where are the b--big people?" Kathy spread her hands, holding them wide.

"I assure you, Miss Taylor, you've the wrong idea about Weatherford." Mrs. Engles' cultured upper-class voice sounded a little snobby. "This is a posh establishment where one comes to work out and relax. We help people find their real self." She started walking again.

Kathy stifled a giggle, thinking the woman definitely had a few marbles loose upstairs. "Well, I sure hope you can find the *real* me in here." She pointed to her chest. "I'd say you've a hell of a job ahead of you."

Mrs. Engles smiled for the first time as she opened the door to Kathy's suite. Kathy had the feeling it was something the woman rarely did. "If anyone can find you, my dear, rest assured the staff at Weatherford can do the job. In four weeks, you'll not recognize the woman you've become." She paused at the door. "Do get some rest tonight, dear. Your program starts in the morning, and Mr. York advised us to put you on a strict routine."

"F--Four weeks? Are you sure?" Kathy had thought this was for only one week.

"That's right, dear. We're going to turn you into a new person."

"Thanks a lot, Devon," Kathy muttered to the closed

door. Was he trying to help her or merely getting her out of the way? She had been taking up a lot of his time. And this whole thing -- had been at his suggestion. Her temper simmered, and then she remembered his kiss. That had not been just a friendly peck. That had been a KISS! Looking down, she saw that chill bumps covered her arms as she started to unpack her clothes. If that were the way he kissed when he was angry, she could well imagine his passionate kiss. Lord, help her to be able to sample both.

For now, however, she would give Devon the benefit of the doubt and try to remember he was trying to help her.

As she put away the last pair of shorts, she recalled Mrs. Engles' words "*strict routine*," and Kathy couldn't help wondering just how strict, strict was. Somehow, she had the feeling she would find out in the morning.

"IT'S TIME TO GET UP," a cheery voice sounded beside her bed. It couldn't be Tina, Kathy thought in her sleep-filled mind because Tina never got up early. Then as if a light bulb clicked on, Kathy remembered she wasn't at home.

"Huh?" she mumbled without lifting her head.

"It's a beautiful day, and the morning is waiting."

Kathy pried open an eye and saw a bright, cheerful, young girl. She had short, brown hair that was cut just above her ears, and she was smiling at her. Unfortunately, Kathy had never been a morning person, and this little pixie was a little too much to take at this hour. "Who the hell are you?"

"My, my, my." The girl smiled, her dimples becoming obvious. "I see we're not a morning person, but --" She reached down and jerked back the covers, "--You'll get accustomed to our routine in a few days." She went over to the basket she had brought with her and pulled out a pair of green shorts and a white tee shirt. "After all, you're paying us a lot of money to help you relax and get you in shape."

Kathy struggled to a sitting position as she watched little Miss Mary Poppins skip into the bathroom and turn on the shower. "I thought I was relaxed until you burst through the door." Kathy slid out of bed and stretched. Feeling dizzy after that little bit of exertion, she promptly sat back down. "I suppose you want me to get ready?"

"That's right. You have five minutes," her new helper informed her as she began to make up the bed. "Don't bother to put on any makeup because you'll just sweat it off."

Kathy stumbled into the bathroom and groped her way into the shower. As the hot water beat down upon her head, each little drop shouted over and over again. *You'll just sweat it off.* "Great," she mumbled. Surely, she'd arrived in hell. As Kathy dried off and slipped on her clothes, she looked heavenward, "Please let me live through today."

Mary Poppins was still waiting when Kathy walked back into the bedroom. Somehow, she knew Miss Poppins would be. "I don't believe I know your name."

"It's Mary Leigh. I'll be your personal trainer while you're at Weatherford, and I hope your friend, too."

Kathy started laughing at the name Mary. To her, she'd always be Mary Poppins.

"I'm going to stick to you like glue." Mary Leigh laughed as she opened the door.

"Wonderful," Kathy mumbled.

They passed the dining area and, of course, Kathy stopped. "Didn't we forget something, Mary Pop--Leigh?"

The perky little girl, who couldn't possibly weigh more than a hundred pounds and probably had never had a weight problem in her life, stopped and turned around. "Like what?"

"Breakfast, of course."

Mary Leigh walked back and took Kathy's hand. "It's not time for breakfast, we've got a five mile hike ahead of us."

"Surely you jest!" Kathy cut her eyes at her new soul mate who was now pulling her out the door and to the beginning of a path. A path, she might add, that looked like Mount Everest minus the snow. "We are going to walk out there . . . in the desert? There are snakes out there."

"It's not that bad. And if you don't bother them, they won't bother you."

"Somehow, Mary Leigh . . ." Kathy let out a long controlled sigh. "I don't feel comforted. I hope somebody told the snakes."

"I've never seen any so I don't think you'll have to worry. We'll have five miles done before you know it."

Kathy frowned. Was five the only number these exercise people knew? "I definitely need to teach you a new number -- like one."

"You're funny, Kathy. I think I'm going to enjoy working with you." Mary Leigh smiled. "You are different from the other clients I've worked with. Come on let's jog for a while."

"Well, you'll change your mind when you have to carry me home."

The crisp morning air felt good on Kathy's face, and the trail they took was really beautiful. And, if the last two miles hadn't been pure hell, Kathy probably would have noticed that fact, but all she could think of was her screaming muscles that wanted to be put out of their misery.

They had jogged and walked and jogged some more until finally Kathy begged to crawl. But Mary Leigh kept prodding her until the very end when she said. "Now that wasn't that bad, was it?"

"We're through?" Kathy looked up from her burning feet and saw the clubhouse just ahead. "I made it," she whispered. Just knowing she hadn't sat down in the middle of the path and called for an ambulance made pride sweep over her.

"Yes, you did. And soon you'll be able to run the entire five miles," Mary Leigh commented as they headed for the pool. "Let's take a swim and cool off." She started for the clubhouse, but stopped upon hearing a splash. Spinning around she began to laugh. "Most people put a bathing suit on first." She began laughing.

Kathy swam to the side of the pool her clothes clinging like glue when she climbed out. The white tennis shoes sloshed with water as she neared Mary Leigh. "It was just too tempting . . . I couldn't wait." Kathy began laughing too. She took the towel Mary Leigh offered. After wiping off her face, Kathy looked behind her and cringed as she noticed several pairs of eyes rested upon her.

The rest of the morning went by in a blur of exercise and rub downs right up until lunch.

They entered the dining room that overlooked a fountain. The tables were covered in lush forest green and bright pink napkins. Huge ferns hung on chains above their heads, and Kathy couldn't help thinking that anyplace this lovely had to have great food.

The waiter appeared at their sides and poured sparkling clear mountain water in their glasses.

"This is good," Kathy remarked, taking another sip.

"And it's good for you."

Kathy looked at all the other tables and frowned. "Didn't the waiter forget to give us the menus?"

Mary Leigh snickered. "You're on a diet. There will be no choosing."

Before Kathy could tell her she'd paid a lot of money for this torture, the waiter arrived and sat a plate in front of them. Laying on a bed of lettuce, was a variety of fresh vegetables. Kathy glanced at her plate. She would think positive and enjoy this appetizer, but the main course had better be damn good.

"Have you worked here long?" Kathy asked.

Mary Leigh spread a napkin out in her lap. "This is my fourth summer. I've found I really enjoy helping people."

Kathy munched on a carrot stick. "You'll probably change your mind after you've worked with me for awhile."

"Well, I admit, so far you've been livelier than the rest." Mary Leigh took a sip of water. "Can I say something?"

Having eaten all the rabbit food, Kathy leaned back in the chair. She was beginning to like Mary Poppins, and she hoped they would become friends.

"Let's get one thing straight from the start," Kathy said. "If we are going to be friends, let's make a promise that we will always say what's on our mind." She reached her hand out.

"Deal." Mary Leigh took her hand. "You are very pretty, Kathy. Why do you try to hide your looks?"

"You really think so?" She watched Mary nod her

head. "Actually, I've never thought of myself as being pretty."

"But you are." Mary Leigh studied Kathy's face before she spoke. "You just don't play up what Mother Nature gave you. Before you leave, we'll teach you many things I think you'll like and find useful."

Kathy looked around, wondering if the waiter had died. "That appetizer was good, but where's the main course?"

"I'm glad you enjoyed it," Mary Leigh said. "Unfortunately --" she took a deep breath then continued. "That was the main course."

Horror filled Kathy's body. Devon had sent her here to die.

CHAPTER 5

*R*ising at the crack of dawn to begin exercising and dragging herself to bed at night had been the worst thing Kathy had ever done. The past two weeks had been a blur. Mary Leigh had kept Kathy busy all day . . . every day and by the end of the first week, she had begged Mary Leigh to shoot her and put her out of her misery. Kathy had not even had time to think of Devon.

Today was Sunday, and she had been given the day off. Taking advantage, she slept until noon, then spent the rest of the afternoon by the pool.

Kathy felt relaxed, but a little homesick when she entered her room and turned on the light beside the bed. Removing her bathing suit, she hung it in the shower then slipped on a kelly-green pair of shorts, and fastened it with a safety pin. Kathy noticed her skin had turned a golden tan, and somehow she even felt healthier.

As she sat on the bed the safety pin popped. Another sign she had been starved to death for the past two weeks. "Damn!" Kathy stood up and refastened the pin. Still her shorts hung loose on her hips. She would need new clothes before she went home. Picking up the phone receiver, Kathy dialed Devon's apartment. She had hoped he would have called her by now. Evidently, it had been out of sight, out of mind.

"Hello." That crisp English accent was just how she remembered it sounding.

"I hope I'm not interrupting."

"Kathy?" Devon paused. "Is that you, Luv?"

"No. It's the carcass of what I use to be. Of course, it is." She laughed. "Have you forgotten my voice so soon?" He sure sounded surprised, she thought.

"Most certainly, I have not," Devon protested. "Damn it's good to hear your voice. How are you doing?"

Kathy thought he sounded sincere, but she wasn't going to let him off so easy. "If you missed talking to me . . ." she attempted to sound sexy. "Why haven't you called?"

"Did you think I did not call by choice?" His voice held a note of irritation as he continued. "I can hear you now. I bet you said out of sight, out of mind. Am I not right?"

Kathy couldn't help but giggle. He knew her so well. "Well what was I supposed to think? Especially after you sent me to hell for four weeks! Four weeks, I'd like to point out, you forgot to mention."

"Did they not tell you?"

"Tell me what?" she asked. "And you still haven't answered my question. Why didn't you call?"

"The school asked that I not phone for the first two weeks, so you could have a chance to adjust," he explained. "I was going to call you next week, but seeing as you've beat me to it . . . How are you doing? Have you settled in?"

"I guess you could say I have." Kathy thought back over her trying days as she twisted the phone cord around her finger. "There have been many times I've lingered near death." She hoped her sad voice made him feel a wee bit guilty. "But good old Mary Leigh just jerked me up by the hair of my head and demanded I get with the program."

"Mary Leigh?"

"She's my jailor."

Devon laughed. "I sure have missed your sense of humor. Has it really been as bad as all that?"

"Not really. Or at least it's better," she admitted. "But four weeks, Devon!"

"I'm sorry, Luv. But you complained so about a week that I assumed if I told you four weeks, I'd never get you on the plane. And I really did have your best interest at heart. Tell me, how much weight have you lost?"

"Fifteen pounds and lots of inches," Kathy boasted. "Needless to say, I haven't seen *real* food in a long time."

"Good girl. I'm proud of you. I knew you could do it." His praise made her feel ten feet high. "But I'd kill for a plate of spaghetti."

"I'll tell you what we'll do. I believe you have a birthday coming up on September fifteenth. I will take you to the Fair and afterward treat you to a small spaghetti dinner."

Boy, did that sound good. Kathy's salivary glands started to water. She couldn't wait. Her two favorite things spaghetti and Devon . . . and she wasn't sure in exactly which order.

"Promise."

"I wouldn't let you down, Luv."

"Oh, I almost forgot the reason I'm calling. I need some new clothes. I guess you could say mine are out-growing me."

"And I thought you phoned because you had longed to hear my voice and couldn't wait another minute," he teased.

"I do miss you." Kathy softly spoke the words she felt. All kidding aside, she missed Devon more than food.

There was a pause as if he waited before he spoke. "I miss you, too, and I'll be damn glad when you come home. Perhaps then I won't work myself to death."

So he did miss her. She couldn't have been happier, but Kathy didn't want him to know just how much she'd wanted his company. From her previous experience, she found once a man knew how much she cared, he usually walked all over her or ran for the hills. She'd be careful this time just in case there was a slim chance with Devon.

"I'll have the money wired to school for you." Devon broke into her thoughts. "Wait a minute. There's someone at the door."

"I guess I better let you go then," Kathy said, reluctant to hang up the phone. "I'll see you in two weeks."

"I'll be there to pick you up. Sweet dreams, Luv."

The phone slipped from her hand. She felt better just talking with him, and Devon really did sound as if he'd missed her. "He misses me," she all but shouted to the room. What she wouldn't give to see him. Kathy signed. She'd keep busy these upcoming weeks and hopefully they would go by quickly.

As she lay her head on the pillow, Kathy speculated on who was at the door. She hoped it was no one of importance and quickly tossed any possibilities out of her mind. Instead, she went over their conversation again. Devon had said they would spend her birthday together. And now she was looking forward to the day now more than ever. She wondered when she returned home if things would be like before? Would Devon spend as much time with her, or would she be like an old shoe and tossed aside.

If only she had a crystal ball.

If only she had more confidence in herself.

She closed her eyes and drifted off to a dreamland where everybody and everything was perfect.

DEVON PITCHED the brief his assistant had dropped by in a large stack of papers. Pulling out his desk chair, he sat down and reached for his checkbook. He smiled as he wrote out the check for Kathy's clothes. He hadn't been joking when he told her how much he'd missed her. Every night he had spent working on cases and sometimes didn't get home before ten o'clock. But no matter how late, Kathy invaded his thoughts before he went to sleep. She was as pure as freshly fallen snow. There didn't seem to be a devious bone in her body. He missed that good feeling he had inside when he was with Kathy. Was he starting to care deeply for her?

He must be. Because tonight when his business partner told him they had an important dinner meeting with Blake and his wife, Devon tried to stand his ground that he would go alone. However, Ed insisted it would be an easier meeting if Devon brought a date so Mrs. Blake would feel more at ease. Ed suggested Whitney. When Devon refused, Ed wanted to know since when had Devon had an aversion to women.

Devon argued. But he'd been so tired from working he finally gave in. He had just hung up from asking Whitney out when Kathy phoned.

God, he felt like a heel! Of course, he had no ties to Kathy and could date whomever he wanted. So why did he feel so darn guilty?

DEVON AND WHITNEY met Ed and the Blakes at the Charter House. They were making headway with Adam Blake, and his wife, Ann, seemed to like Whitney from the start.

Ed leaned over and whispered to Devon. "You're a fool not to marry Whitney. Look at what an asset she would be to you."

Devon didn't bother to comment. What Ed said rang true. Whitney was beautiful and knew how to handle herself around clients. Maybe one day she might be the one he considered marrying, but not now.

After his third glass of Scotch, Devon leaned back in his chair. Whitney slid her hand under his arm and moved closer to him. Since all the business had been conducted, Devon was tired and ready to go. He looked at Whitney. "I think we should call it a night." He would have to be a fool not to notice the seductive way she looked at him.

Another pair of eyes watched Devon as he left with Whitney. Tina smiled and leaned over the table to speak to her girlfriend. "Well, Well, it seems while the cat's away the mouse will play. I wondered if he truly cared for Kathy. And I just received my answer."

When they reached her apartment, Devon stopped at the door. "You're not spending the night, darling?" Whitney asked.

"Not tonight, Whitney."

"But Devon, you always stay with me." She looked puzzled. "What has changed?"

"Nothing."

Whitney glared at him. "It's that girl!"

"Perhaps." Devon didn't bother to deny her accusations.

"You don't love her, Devon. You merely pity the wretched thing."

Devon's body tensed at the insult. "I didn't say I loved Kathy. But," he bit out. "I do feel something for her, and I intend to find out just what that something is. And you're wrong if you have any delusions that I merely pity, Kathy." Devon stared at Whitney, realizing suddenly that her beauty was merely superficial. "As I said, it's time for us not only to say good night but to call it quits!"

"I don't believe you, Devon!" Whitney shook her head as her eyes brimmed with tears. "You'll never be happy with that fat thing. You've seen the way she dresses. Why didn't you invite her tonight . . . I'll tell you why . . . it's because you're ashamed of her."

"Good night, Whitney." Devon turned and walked away.

"You'll be back," she taunted before she closed the door. "You'll be back."

KATHY DECIDED to wait until the last week to buy her clothes. The exercising had gotten easier, and she could definitely see the results of her hard work. No longer did she have a double chin. And she was beginning to discover a waistline.

Her stomach rumbled, a small reminder that she was hungry, so she decided to get a drink. When she passed the candy machine something caught her attention. There in the left-hand corner was one pack of Whoppers. Kathy stopped. Her eyes fixed like glue to the cream-colored package. Quickly, she looked around to make sure nobody was coming. They would never know, Kathy assured her conscience . . . One small pack couldn't hurt. Taking, two quarters and a nickel out of her pocket, she started to place the change in the machine, but the nickel slipped from her fingers and fell to the ground. Crawling around on her knees, she finally found the missing coin. She blew off the dirt and placed it in the slot.

"Let me see. I need to press 'D' ten." Carefully she punched the buttons. The silver screw started to turn -- once -- twice -- then it stopped, never completing the third turn.

"You can't do this to me!" Kathy placed both her hands on the glass and begged the contraption. But the malted milk balls hung in the middle refusing to fall. She felt doomed. Cheated. Deprived.

Kathy beat on the machine with the palms of her hands. "Damn you!" She hauled off and kicked the brown culprit, which had her food and nearly broke her toe in the process.

"Is there some trouble here?" Mary Leigh walked up behind Kathy.

There was no way Kathy could talk her way out of this one. She knew she must look guilty clinging to the machine with both hands. "Trouble? I--I don't think so." Kathy slowly let go of the contraption. "I just came to get a drink."

"Then why are you standing in front of this vending machine?"

"Why?" Kathy hedged. She had better think of something good. She moved over to the drink box. With her back still to Mary Leigh, Kathy slipped her money in the drink machine before answering. "Why? Because I lost a contact," she shut her eye and turned around to stare at Mary Leigh through the other.

The councilor smiled, but if she suspected Kathy was lying, Mary Leigh didn't let on. Instead she simply took her by the arm and said. "In that case, I'll help you back to your room. We have a lot of things to do."

KATHY PURCHASED SEVERAL SUMMER OUTFITS. And today Mary Leigh was helping her work on her make up. She would find Kathy's best features and show her how to play them up. Yeah, sure, Kathy thought as she relaxed in the beauty chair gazing at her image in the mirror.

"I want you to wear this brown eye shadow, and we'll put just a hint of gold under the brow." Mary Leigh handed her a brush. "After all, you are becoming a new person so you need a new look."

Kathy followed her instructions to the letter. Marveling at how different she looked with each new thing they tried.

"You have beautiful eyes," Mary Leigh commented. "They remind me of a cat."

"I must admit they look a lot different since we've put on this shade of eye color. It's amazing what a little bit of makeup will do." Kathy batted her long black lashes flirtatiously for practice.

"It's all in knowing what to do with what you've got." Mary Leigh laughed. "I bet your boyfriend will like this."

"I'm not too sure I have a boyfiend." Kathy wondered what Devon's reactions would be.

"But--" Mary Leigh paused with a puzzled look on her face. "I thought that's who sent you here."

"My aunt's attorney made the arrangements for me to come to Weatherford."

"The way your eyes light up, I have a feeling you'd like him to be more than a business acquaintance."

Kathy smiled. "You wouldn't hear any objections on my end. He's wonderful," she sighed.

"Tell me what he's like."

"Devon is an Englishman. He's tall, has dark hair and brown eyes."

"Sounds yummy."

"Oh, he is." Kathy nodded her head. "He's the spitting image of Pierce Brosnan."

"Who?"

"Remington Steele."

Mary Leigh's eyes grew wide. "You're kidding. How do you take your eyes off him?"

"It isn't easy."

"Well, he must think a lot of you to send you here."

Kathy met her eyes in the mirror. "It isn't exactly like that. I've been left a good sum of money with a stipulation that I must fit into a size eight dress. Do you think I'll make it?"

"Of course, I do. Providing you use a little will power. And remember the drink machine from the candy machine.

"Then, I'm doomed."

"Look. Here's Nina." A tall blond woman came in and stood directly behind Kathy.

"What do you think?" Mary Leigh asked the new girl.

"You did a great job on the makeup, honey. Now let's do that hair."

"Nina is going to give you a new style. With your permission, that is."

Kathy nodded.

Nina walked all around Kathy studying her from every angle. "I like your hair long, honey, but I think we should cut a few layers here and touch the ends with gold to bring out your eyes." Nina rubbed her chin as she thought. "And we'll feather it around your face. What do you think, honey?"

"I think anything would be an improvement or, perhaps, a miracle." They all laughed and the beautician went to work.

Kathy watched as Nina worked her magic. And when she had finished, Kathy couldn't believe the results. She was almost as pretty as her sister. What would Devon think of her now?

"LADIES AND GENTLEMEN, we'll be landing in ten minutes. Please fasten your seat belts." The pilot's voice echoed around the plane.

Kathy was on her way home. She couldn't believe her four weeks in hell were over. Reluctantly she admitted she'd had a good time and made a new friend to boot. She had promised to keep in touch with Mary Leigh.

Kathy also looked a little different than when she had left New Orleans. Her new skirt outfit made her feel very stylish, and it was three dress sizes smaller.

Devon had not called before she left. But he had said he would pick her up, and she couldn't wait to see him.

The wheels bumped as they touched the runway, and her stomach churned with either butterflies or hunger, she wasn't sure which. Just a few more minutes . . . and she would see him. As much as she tried to caution herself she'd probably get hurt, Kathy's heart didn't seem to listen. She was falling for the man fast and hard.

Finally, the door opened, and Kathy started up the jetway to the waiting room. She didn't see Devon at first so she scanned the crowd. Where was he? He couldn't possibly forget . . . could he?

"Hello gorgeous." A voice sounded behind her. "Looking for someone?" Kathy's heart beat loudly as she swung around only to find a pilot flirting with her.

Her smile instantly faded. "Yes, I am."

"Well, he sure is a lucky devil."

Kathy should be flattered, but all she wanted to do was cry. Then she heard a familiar voice.

"Kathy! Kathy! Over here."

Turning she saw her sister and headed in her direction.

"Tina. This is a surprise."

Tina hugged her then stepped back. "I almost didn't recognize you. Just look at how you've changed."

Kathy smiled and swung around. "What do you think?"

"I think I need to go to Weatherford. You look great! Come on let's get your bags."

"Where is Devon? I thought he was picking me up."

"He asked me to come and get you. Devon said he didn't have time, but he would see you later."

Kathy felt all her enthusiasm slowly draining away as they stepped on the escalator, heading for the baggage pickup. Devon didn't have time. She might have missed him, but evidently, he hadn't given her much thought. It was dark outside and after business hours so what could have been so important?

Tina chatted all the way home about her new boyfriend, but Kathy only heard half of what she said.

Why did she give her heart so freely only to have it stepped on? You'd think she would learn.

Heading straight for her room, Kathy began to unpack. She wouldn't think about Devon. She would cast him from her thoughts as easily as he had her.

It should have felt good to be home, but it didn't. Even Tina acted like she'd missed her. She had even volunteered to cook dinner. Kathy would gladly have starved if Devon had shown up.

The doorbell rang.

CHAPTER 6

"*I*'ll get it," Kathy shouted to her sister. "I don't know what you're cooking, but it sure smells great."

"It's a surprise," Tina yelled from the kitchen.

Kathy opened the door then froze. So he decided to make an appearance. She had dreamed about him for weeks, and now he stood before her dressed in a white shirt and navy blue trousers, his tie pulled loose, and his hair wind-blown. As usual, she could do nothing but stare.

Devon couldn't move. Was this his Kathy? The hair was different. It seemed to float around her shoulders and shimmer as if the sun had painted gold streaks through every strand, and her complexion was darker than before, but her lips were still the soft pink that he remembered. And those amber eyes . . . At first he read surprise in them, but it had quickly changed to a look of irritation. Hadn't she missed him?

"Hello, Luv." Devon smiled. "Where's my welcome home hug?" He pulled Kathy into his arms and immediately felt her stiffen.

Holding her away from him, he asked. "What's wrong?"

"I didn't say anything was wrong," she snapped. "What are you doing here?"

"What the bloody hell is bothering you!" Devon had not slept in the past twenty-four hours, and his temper was short.

Startled, Kathy stepped back; Devon had never raised his voice to her. This wasn't how she had pictured her homecoming at all. But she was angry at being stood up, and wasn't about to let the matter rest. "I thought you were going to pick me up at the airport?"

"Didn't Tina tell you why I couldn't come?"

"Oh, she told me!" Kathy folded her arms in front of her. "She said you were busy and would see me later . . . more than likely at your convenience. I'm glad to see you could fit me into your schedule so soon."

"Do you mind if I come in?" Of course, he didn't wait for her reply, but merely slammed the door behind him before walking toward her. Kathy took a tentative step backward until she felt the wall behind her. Devon placed a hand just above her left shoulder and blocked her with his body so she couldn't move. She was trapped.

"If losing weight is going to turn you into a bloody shrew, I'd just as soon you didn't lose another ounce." His vivid brown eyes told her he was dead serious. "I don't believe your sister conveyed the message the way I sent it."

"Really," Kathy managed to choke out. She was squeezed like a trapped mouse between the wall and Devon. He was too close, and that angry spark in the depth of his eyes made him seem more virile, if that were possible. God help her, she was going to hyperventilate right there. Somebody get a bag!

"I believe . . ." He paused and took a deep breath. "I asked Tina to convey how disappointed I was that I couldn't pick you up personally, but . . . one of my clients was in jail and I had to get him out. I thought you would understand, and I'd see you tonight. I guess it was silly of me to think such a thing."

Kathy tugged at her bottom lip with her teeth. A part of her wanted to smile because he hadn't stood her up, yet a part of her wanted to choke Tina for leading her to believe differently. When Devon was this near her thoughts just seemed to turn to lust, draining her anger away. "I'm sorry I misunderstood, but you would have felt the same way."

His head moved closer, and Kathy shut her eyes in anticipation. How many nights had she dreamed of Devon's kisses? She breathed in his British Sterling fragrance and felt the heat from his body as she tilted her head up to meet his lips.

"Break that up." Tina interrupted as the doorbell rang. "That must be John."

Kathy ducked under Devon's arm and went into the living room. Willing her heart to slow down to second gear, she let her breath out. Why couldn't she have been an only child? Then she wouldn't have these problems. Kathy wondered if Devon was feeling the same disappointment she did. She sneaked a peek but couldn't tell by looking at him. He had pulled his tie loose and unbuttoned the collar of his white shirt that contrasted against his brown skin, giving him an aura of sensuality. She held her hand out for the tie. His fingers brushed hers, causing her heart to hammer wildly, but she managed to take the tie and lay it across the chair.

Tina walked in with a fellow who looked like he'd just

stepped off the beach. His sandy blonde hair was long, and his muscles bulged beneath this shirt.

"John, I'd like you to meet my sister, Kathy and her lawyer-friend, Devon York."

They exchanged pleasantries, and Tina announced dinner was ready. Kathy wondered where Tina had found this good-looking hunk. Men just seemed to fall at her sister's feet.

Devon held the chair out for Kathy then took the seat next to her. Kathy stared at the feast set before her. Tina had prepared red beans and rice, French bread, crab gumbo and chocolate pie. Food . . . real food! Now was her chance. Kathy's taste buds went into high gear. But when the dishes were passed a miracle occurred. Weatherford had drummed moderation into her head. She had been brainwashed, Kathy thought as she took a small portion of gumbo and half a slice of bread.

"Is that all you're going to eat?" Tina asked, the astonishment ringing clear in her voice.

Kathy felt her cheeks grow warm especially since she'd just met John. He probably thought she was a first class pig. "I--I've learned to eat less. Besides, I still have a long ways to go," she murmured.

"Yes, you do." Tina laughed and turned to John. "I should explain, sweetheart, so you're not in the dark. Kathy used to be fatter than she is now. She has just returned from a swanky resort were they have done wonders for her."

Devon had remained quiet over the tempting feast Tina had prepared, but he had just about had enough of her putting Kathy down. He'd met too many superficial women like Tina. They were all alike, never caring for anyone's feelings but their own. "Tina, perhaps you should try Weatherford. You never can tell . . . they might even help someone like you."

"Huh?" Tina's eyes grew wide and her face flushed scarlet all the while she tried to pretend Devon hadn't insulted her. "Maybe I'll get to go there one day," she murmured.

Kathy glanced at Devon and bit her lip to keep from laughing. Her heart grew a size larger. He had taken up for her; nobody had ever done that before. Maybe there was a chance for them. Just maybe.

When the chocolate pie passed by, Kathy resisted and had a cup of coffee. As they sat around talking, Devon reached under the table and took her hand in his. His strong fingers wrapped protectively around hers, and he gave her a reassuring squeeze.

Warmth spread throughout Kathy's body as she pressed her hand within his strong grip. Yet she knew she shouldn't read anything into this simple gesture. His expression never changed as he carried on the conversation. They were friends . . . nothing more.

The evening ended much too soon for Kathy. She walked out into the warm night with Devon. A slight breeze brought the smell of jasmine and moonlight as Devon leaned back against his car.

"It's good to have you home, Kathy."

"Thank you for coming tonight." She paused. "I'm sorry about my earlier confusion." Seeing the fatigue around his eyes, Kathy reached up and touched his cheek. "You look tired. I think you've been working too much."

"I am a wee bit weary. I've not had any sleep since yesterday." Devon reached up and placed his hand on hers, shutting his eyes for just a moment. "One of my associates is a bit laid up in the hospital, and Ed and I have had to split his case load."

Kathy's stomach tightened. She stared at his firm sensual mouth. He appeared so vulnerable that she longed to hold him. "I guess I won't be seeing much of you then?"

"Probably not." He still held her hand, but he guided it around his cheek and kissed her palm. "I'll still make the time for our trips to the spa. After all we have a goal for you to achieve."

Kathy's compassion evaporated instantly. "I forgot." She couldn't stop the disappointment in her voice. "I'm work too."

All too quickly she felt herself crushed against Devon's hard chest as his arms wrapped around her. "I don't want to fight, Kathy."

She looked up at him. He stared at her upturned face for a long time. If only she could read his thoughts.

"I honestly don't know what you are to me. It's true you're part of a job, but I think there is more to it than that," he whispered. "God, how I've missed you."

Before she could say anything, Devon lowered his head and captured her mouth. The warm night air wrapped around them in a gentle breeze while Devon's fingers roamed possessively across her back. His lips moved with alarming expertise, and soon Kathy became intoxicated with the many sensations he produced within her body.

His mouth was warm, tender and giving. Kathy slipped her fingers into his dark hair, and instantly he tightened his arms around her as his lips moved on hers with fierce hunger. Devon pulled her hips against his thighs, and she instantly became aware of the effect she had on him.

What was she doing? This is what she wanted, yet she

was afraid. Kathy didn't want to be on his list of many or a one-night stand. She wanted commitment. She wanted Devon to love her. If she fell willingly into his arms now, what would he think of her?

Kathy never got the chance to ponder the point or to say anything. Devon broke off the kiss, leaving her momentarily stunned. However, he didn't push her away in disgust, he merely held her tenderly with his cheek resting on top of her head.

She could hear the wild thumping of Devon's heart as he gently stroked her back. What she wouldn't give to know what he was thinking. Did he already have regrets? Or did he truly care? Kathy couldn't believe that Devon could love her. Hadn't he said that he honestly didn't know what she meant to him? The next time she fell in love it had to be with someone she could trust . . . someone who would love her no matter what shape she came in . . . someone who would love her for herself.

Her mind screamed for him to say something. Anything! Why couldn't she play hard-to-get like most women? Instead she was content just being held by Devon. God, she was a pushover.

"Kathy, I don't know what we have here," he whispered huskily. "Let's take it slow. I don't want to have any regrets down the line."

IN THE WEEKS THAT FOLLOWED, their relationship took a strange turn. Devon had said he wanted to move slow. Slow . . . he'd all but stopped. As far as Kathy was concerned a snail could move faster.

True to his word, Devon stayed busy, and the only time

Kathy saw him was their daily trips to the exercise spa and dinner.

Before long it was the middle of September and Kathy grew bored. She hadn't had any luck finding a job, which didn't seem to bother Devon one bit when she complained. He seemed to think she didn't need to work.

Tina had been in New York for the last month, but when she returned she once again took over the cooking and Kathy found herself weakening.

She didn't think she'd fudged too much until she stepped on the scales at the spa. The needle marked a five-pound gain, and she dreaded looking at Devon who looked ready to breathe fire.

"Uh oh."

"That's all you have to say!" Devon frowned at her, his disappointment evident in every feature.

"I've probably been eating too much."

"At least you know what the problem is," Devon said curtly, then he left her to start his weight lifting.

Embarrassed by Devon's rudeness, Kathy made her way to the rowing machine. He didn't understand. How could he? He'd probably never had a weight problem in his life. So how could he understand her weakness. Devon was always in control -- perfect. She hated it. And at the moment she wasn't too fond of him either.

Kathy worked at her exercise program with vengeance. With each stroke of the rowing machine, her anger grew. With each turn of the bicycle, she vowed to give Devon a piece of her mind.

But when the time came, they drove home in silence with Kathy staring out the window. It was so quiet, the turn signal sounded like a loud bell when Devon turned into her driveway.

As the Jag came to a standstill at her front door, Kathy waited for Devon to come around and let her out. At least, he was a gentleman; she'd give him that. What else would she expect from somebody who was perfect? She stepped out and murmured, "Thanks for taking me." Not bothering to look at him, she started for the house.

It seemed Devon had other ideas as he reached out and caught her arm. "Wait a minute."

Kathy turned and leveled an icy gaze at him.

Devon saw the coldness in her eyes. The sparkling anger turned her eyes to twenty-four-Karat gold. Kathy really was beautiful, no matter how hard she tried to hide the fact. She was beautiful. Letting go of her, he folded his arms across his chest. He was only trying to help her. Couldn't she see that? She had been doing too well to start slipping back into her bad habits. What was she hiding from? It had to be more than hurt from a previous boyfriend. Somewhere along the way, she had convinced herself she was worthless, and he intended to change that fact before December.

"I'm sorry I snapped at you earlier. But we've worked so hard -- I don't want to see you forfeit everything."

"For God sakes, Devon. It was just a few pounds, and I still have two months. And it is *my* body."

"But I happen to care about that body. And about you," he admitted, then added, "A few pounds here and a few pounds there will soon add up."

"I guess you're right." Kathy shrugged her shoulders. "But when I see all that good food; it's hard to pass it up."

"Especially if you have a lovely sister who keeps shoving it at you."

"She's not really that bad." Kathy felt she had to take up for her sister.

Devon gave her a doubtful frown. "I think you need your own place."

Kathy's eyes grew wide. "Perhaps, I do. But I don't have a job, or should I point that small fact out to you."

"You have pointed that fact out to me several times in the last month. I repeat, you don't have to work."

"But, I'm bored. I need something to do."

"Precisely why I'm suggesting that you need your own place," he said thoughtfully. "I think you should move into your aunt's old house." He saw her mouth pop open in surprise. "It has lots of character and can use some tender loving care. I offered to buy it from your aunt once, but she wanted to save it for you."

"For me?" Kathy placed a hand on her chest and repeated. "My aunt's house." She grew quiet for a moment as she conjured up a picture of the place. "I remember going there when I was a child. The place is huge."

"It's a nice sized estate and will keep you busy fixing it up. Just think of the exercise you'll get cleaning it."

"Thanks a lot." She frowned at him. Did the man always think of her weight? Did he look at her and see a blob? "What did you do before you had my weight loss program to keep you busy?"

"Believe it or not." He shrugged. "Life was pretty dull before you dropped into my office." Devon studied her. "Haven't you ever wanted a place of your own, Luv? Where you can call the shots. Aren't you tired of being under your sister's thumb?"

Kathy stiffened. "You don't like, Tina, do you?"

"I don't like the way she treats you." Devon reached for Kathy, and his arms encircled her rigid body. "You deserve better, and I intend to see that you get it." He ran his thumb over her chin."

"Thank you for caring." Kathy said as she stared at his chest. Would she see sympathy in his eyes and nothing more? Would she ever hear the word love from him?

"Oh, Luv, I do care a great deal for you." His thumb traced a path to her ear, and Kathy shivered. I've tried to block you out of my thoughts at work only to have your face sneak back into my mind," he murmured.

"Devon." Kathy stared into his eyes. "Don't say these things if you don't mean them." She held her breath. Was he trying to say he cared?

"I do . . ." Devon murmured as his lips descended to hers, " . . . mean every word."

His husky voice made Kathy's head swim. When his tongue touched her trembling lips she parted them easily to let him slip through. She couldn't stop the moan that rose in her throat. God, this man made her melt. He turned her into a quivering mass of jelly. His arms tightened possessively. She had never felt so protected, so loved, and so helpless. Should she trust him and let her heart go? Or was this a game to Devon? Let's help the little fat girl. No. He couldn't kiss her like he was doing if he didn't care for her just a little.

All the warning bells went off in Devon's head. Don't get involved with your client they warned him, but the minute Kathy's arms went around his neck he deepened his kiss. Devon liked the way she felt in his arms. He liked the French perfume she wore. And he more than enjoyed the pleasurable sensation that raced through his blood when she pressed intimately against his body. He was driving himself half mad with desire, and it was becoming more and more difficult to stop with a mere kiss. They were getting ready to swim into deep water. And the one big question was -- was that what they both wanted?

Devon raised his head. His eyes never leaving her swollen lips. "I must say, Luv, you sure do that very well."

"Thank you," she murmured. "I had a good teacher," she teased.

Devon tensed. His eyes left her lips to move to Katherine's laughing gold eyes. He knew she teased him, but he didn't particularly like the thoughts that another man had held her like he was doing. And another man had had the same lustful thoughts that he had now. Yet, he knew he had no rights to her, so he quickly squelched the jealously that rose like a demon.

He kissed the end of her nose. "Tomorrow is your birthday. What better day to have you move into your own place."

"You remembered my birthday?" Something flickered in the depths of her eyes. "You haven't said anything in so long I thought you'd forgotten."

"Of course, I remembered," Devon replied with a smile. "And tomorrow will be your day. After we get you settled in, we'll go to the fair and then have that glorious dinner I promised you. And I won't mention your diet the entire night."

"Are you sure?" Kathy had her doubts.

"I promise." He held up his hand.

"Spaghetti, wine, and you." She took a deep breath. "I don't know which one will be the best."

Devon chuckled then gave her another quick kiss before walking around to his side of the car. Just before he ducked in, he looked at her with a wicked gleam in his eyes. "Tomorrow night, remind me to ask which you liked best when the night is finished."

Kathy watched as he drove away rooted to the stop

where she stood. Her temperature soared from 98.6 degrees to boiling. Was he suggesting a *very* romantic evening? His voice definitely held a promise . . .

God, she was going to faint!

CHAPTER 7

*A*fter a good hot shower, Kathy climbed underneath the cool sheets. She rolled on her left side and reached for the lamp switch to turn it off. Now she was prepared for wonderful dreams of Devon.

She pictured the dress she'd wear and heard all the witty conversation she'd keep him entertained with. He'd laugh and smile and finally tell her she was the love of his life.

"Yeah, right," she mumbled as her eyelids popped open. The large red numbers on the digital clock read 1:30 a.m. She sighed and rolled over to her right side and once again contemplated sleep.

Would Devon spend more time with her when she had her own house? She could picture cooking dinner for him then curling up on the sofa to watch a movie. What a nice thought.

Turning over on her back, Kathy stared at the shadows flickering on the ceiling. Maybe Devon wouldn't do anything, but take her out to eat. She bit the side of her lip.

And what would happen in December if she did meet her goal? Would he walk out of her life . . . forever?

"Damn!" She sat straight up in bed. Now the red numerals read 3:30 a.m. What would it take for her to have a little confidence? Evidently, there would be no sleeping tonight.

"In that case, I'll just start packing," Kathy declared to the empty room. She slid out of bed and flipped on the light.

By seven o'clock everything was packed in suitcases or stacked in boxes except for one last item. As Kathy attempted to take the picture off the wall, it slipped from her grasp and crashed to the floor sending slivers of glass flying everywhere.

"What a mess," Kathy muttered as she shook her head and frowned at the shattered mess. Carefully, she slipped on her bedroom shoes and started for the door to get the vacuum cleaner, but when she opened the door, she squealed and jumped back.

"Would you like to tell me why you're making all this God-awful racket so early in the morning?" Tina demanded though a yawn.

"Good morning, sis." Kathy brushed past her. When she got to the hall closet, she opened the door and pulled out the machine. "I was taking a picture down and it slipped." Kathy came back to her room. "Sorry, I woke you."

"You should be." Tina yawned and blinked her eyes several times. "What is this?" She swept her hands around the room. "Planning on going somewhere?"

Kathy grasped the plug and started to pull the cord out of the vacuum. "I've decided it's time to get my own place."

Tina looked at her suspiciously. "Just like that. You've decided to move. Were you going to tell me or just sneak out?"

"Don't be silly." Kathy bent over and plugged in the machine. "And be careful there's glass everywhere," she warned before looking at her sister again. "Of course, I was going to tell you this morning at breakfast. if figured you'd be happy to be rid of me."

"Thank you, for letting me know so soon. What if I wanted to get another roommate to help with the bills?"

Kathy felt a twinge of guilt as she glanced at her sister. "I never thought about that."

"That's your biggest problem, Kathy," Tina snapped. She moved away from the door and started for the bench at the end of the bed. "You never think."

"Well, I couldn't have told you any sooner," Kathy defended herself. "Because I didn't decide until last night."

"Ouch!" Tina screamed as she jerked up her foot. "Get some tissue quick before I get blood on the floor!" She hopped the rest of the way to the bench.

"If you just decided last night --" Tina took the Kleenex from Kathy and pressed it against her foot. "Where are you going to live?"

"In Aunt Catherine's house."

"Devon!" Tina's head jerked up with an all-knowing look in her eyes. "I might have known he would have something to do with this."

Kathy propped her hand on her hip. "What do you mean by that remark?"

"He is constantly controlling your life."

Kathy felt the heat in her cheeks. She was tired of Tina putting Devon down and acting like the righteous, older sister. Come to think of it, Kathy was tired of Tina. "He is not."

"Isn't he?" Tina's brow raised in question. "First, he has you fired, then he sends you to the fat farm. Every day he takes you to exercise, and now he's moving you where *he* wants you!"

"He's trying to help me. That's all." Not wanting to hear anymore, Kathy picked up the vacuum cleaner wand to the machine.

"Why? What's in it for him?"

Kathy looked over her shoulder. "You have a devious mind. Devon is a friend."

"Has it occurred to you, sister dear, that until a few months ago you had never even heard of Devon York? He didn't become your friend until he was forced to." Tina's voice was heavy with sarcasm. "And the prospect of a million dollars probably has a great deal to do with his friendship."

Kathy knew the tears that were building in her eyes would escape at any moment. "I don't want to talk about this anymore. I'm sure you'll be happy once I'm gone." She turned her back on Tina and flipped on the vacuum switch.

"That's right, Kathy," Tina shouted above the noise. "Bury your head in the sand. But you know I'm right." Tina hopped to the door. "And if you can get up the nerve, ask Mr. Wonderful what he did while he had you safely tucked away at the Weatherford."

DEVON ARRIVED MIDMORNING DRESSED CASUALLY in jeans and a ruby-red shirt. It was a sin for any one man to look so delicious, Kathy thought as she loaded the last box into her car.

Tina had gone to her room and hadn't come out to say goodbye. Kathy wasn't sure how she felt about Tina's obvious sulk. Perhaps disappointed, yet a part of her was still angry with Tina. Kathy looked back at the apartment. "I guess that's everything."

"Good." Devon slammed the trunk lid. "Do you want to say goodbye to your sister? Or is she even here?"

"Yes, she's here." Kathy hesitated, torn by conflicting emotions. "She wasn't too pleased with the news I was leaving."

"I don't imagine so." Devon's voice was calm, his gaze steady. "You're taking the first step to independence today, Luv. And I've the feeling you just might prove to be the strongest sister by far." He opened the door and Kathy slid into her car, smiling at his praise.

"Allow me to lead the way to your new home, M'Lady." Devon gave a sweeping bow.

Kathy laughed at Devon's gallant behavior. What would she do without him? "After you, Sir Knight." She watched in the rear view mirror as he walked to his car.

He sure was in a good mood. It was as if he were going out of his way to make her birthday very happy. She hoped that all Tina's accusations about Devon were false. Tina was just jealous that Devon didn't fall for her right away like other men usually did.

They backed out of the driveway, then Kathy followed the green Jag, her thoughts on the driver. Devon wasn't like any man she'd ever known. Thank God, she laughed for she had known some real jerks. His consideration amazed her and he always seemed to put her first. If Devon was acting, then he should win an Oscar because he definitely had her convinced she was special.

Devon smiled as he glanced in the rear-view mirror to make sure Kathy was still following him. He was glad she was taking her first step to independence. Of course, he'd had to give her a little nudge, but he felt this was best for her. Catherine would have been pleased that Kathy was moving into her home and he was glad now he'd agreed to help. However, there were times when he felt like he was helping himself just as much as he was helping Kathy. If that made any sense.

Whistling, Devon admitted he felt light-hearted. This morning when he slid out of bed he'd been assaulted with the urgent need to see Kathy. He wanted to touch her just to make sure she wasn't some wonderful figment of his imagination. As he glanced once more in the mirror, he realized she was for real. . . his genuine, one of a kind, Kathy.

Arriving at Aunt Catherine's place, Kathy stared at the two-story brick house. It was a modest home nothing elaborate. No wonder she had never thought of Aunt Catherine as being wealthy. Come to think of it, she'd never driven a fancy car either. Had her aunt saved every penny for her? Guilt washed over Kathy leaving her cold inside, but this would be her new home, and perhaps she would find out more about her aunt.

When they entered the house, somehow, Kathy felt like she was dreaming. Her home. Her very own home. Someplace where she could make the decisions. She turned. The sunlight sneaked in through the windows and cast a glow over Devon. She felt her heart flutter as she imagined Devon carrying her over the threshold, letting her body slide down his while he planted hot kisses on her mouth. If that happened she probably would die on the spot, but as least she'd die with a smile on her face.

What away to go!

Soon the cars were unloaded and they began pulling sheets off the furniture and opening windows to air out the house. Devon volunteered to vacuum while Kathy dusted.

She was looking around to see what else had to be done when Devon walked up behind her and put his hands on her shoulders. "That's enough work for today, Luv. Let's go to the County Fair."

"Sounds good to me."

As soon as they got out of the car, the aroma of peanuts, hot dogs, pizza, and cotton candy enticed Kathy senses. "I'm not so sure this is a good idea." Her footsteps faltered.

Devon swung his head around and looked at her with a puzzled look in his eyes.

"Can't you smell all that delicious food?" She pointed at the gate. "It might be dangerous if you take me in there."

Devon grinned. "I'll take my chances." He took her by the arm and headed for the admissions' gate. "Perhaps, lunch will soothe the savage beast."

"I could eat a horse."

They walked through the exhibits first. The rumble of the crowd and children's laughter brought a smile to Kathy's face. She didn't know when she'd been so happy. She also realized she didn't know much about Devon, but what she did, she liked very, very well. Unfortunately, her heart was fast overruling her common sense where he was concerned. If she were dreaming, she never wanted to wake up.

"Look." Devon pointed to a small stand. "There are our appetizers."

Kathy knew it had to be fried dough drenched in powdered sugar until her eyes landed to where Devon had pointed. "A pickle?"

"We'll take two," Devon told the vendor. "Not just any pickle, but a kosher dill pickle." Devon handed her one. "Only the best will do for you, Luv."

"Boy, do you know how to charm a lady," she teased, then added. "You did say appetizer?"

"Quite right."

They continued through the many exhibits until they came to the art gallery where Kathy discovered that Devon had an interest in art.

"I think you paint better than what I see in here."

"Thank you," she murmured.

"I do believe you're going to like my birthday present."

She was caught off guard by his sudden announcement. He'd not mentioned her birthday all day. "A present."

He grinned.

"What did you get me?"

"You'll have to wait until tonight to find out."

"That's not fair." Kathy folded her arms across her chest. "Don't tempt me and then not tell me what it is."

"Why not?" Devon's eyes gleamed with a double meaning. "You tempt me every day, Luv."

Kathy smiled at his boyish charm, unsure of what to

say. She tempted him? Hey, she wanted to hear more, but he didn't let her speak. Instead, he reached down and grabbed her hand. "Let's try some rides."

They rode the roller coaster where Kathy snuggled close to Devon, squeezing his hand and praying she'd live through the ride. Then they rode the ferris wheel. She didn't know if it were the rides or Devon that were producing the thousand butterflies fluttering in her stomach, but she sure felt giddy. Finally, they came to the tilt-a-whirl. At least she could keep her feet on the ground with this ride. Devon handed the man their tickets and climbed onto the seat, pulling the black bar down. Devon slid his arm around her. "Are you ready, Luv?"

There was a lot to be said about rides -- *be still my heart*. Kathy smiled before answering, "I sure am. And try not to scream so much this time." She teased him before resting her head on his shoulder. She heard his deep chuckle.

The ride started spinning them round and round. Kathy squealed in delight as the ride threw her against Devon's chest again and again. His arm tightened around her. "I haven't felt like a kid in years," she confessed.

Devon laid his cheek on top of Kathy's head. God, he was happy. He liked Kathy. He liked her a lot. They had absolutely nothing in common, but a will and a crazy Aunt with a wish. But every day Kathy was becoming more and more a part of his life. He couldn't remember when he'd had such a good time. Devon could relax with Kathy. He glanced at her. She had never looked lovelier than when she was laughing. What a beautiful sound.

Kathy opened her eyes and caught him staring at her with his odd expression.

"What's wrong?" she asked.

Devon opened his mouth to respond, but this wild attraction he had to her stepped in. He pulled Kathy to him and lightly brushed her lips. The urge to devour her mouth and express his desire were strong, but now was not the time or place. "There's nothing wrong, Luv." He almost smiled at that small lie. "Would you like to play a few games?"

Kathy nodded. She hadn't missed the desire she saw in his eyes before he covered it up again, and she wondered what would happen tonight when they were alone. Perhaps, they would find paradise.

At the shooting galley, Devon won Kathy a big, white bear. While he took another shot, she wandered over to the goodies booth. She planned to be back before he was finished.

"What are you doing?"

Kathy jumped at the familiar voice behind her. "I want a candy apple."

"Must I always point out the obvious? It's not on your diet."

"I don't care!"

Devon reached over her shoulder and snatched the apple from her fingers. "I'll take that."

"Come on, Devon." She tried to get it from him. "I've killed people for less. I want a bite of that damn apple!" Devon smiled and held the apple away while he teased her. "What if you lived in a country where millions of people were starving."

"I live in a country where one person is starving -- mainly me." Kathy pointed to herself. "It's my birthday. You promised."

"So I did." He chuckled and handed her the apple,

taking the bear, he tucked it under his arm. "Let's go sit on the grass."

They moved out of the main walkway under a large oak tree. Devon slipped his arm around Kathy. "I love it when you get hysterical." He kissed her on the forehead. "That apple does look good. Let me have a bite."

She held the apple up for him. Seeing the red sugar remaining on his lips, she longed to reach up and kiss it off. She wasn't sure how long she looked at Devon, but finally she realized he was speaking to her again.

"Huh?"

"The apple." His gentle nudge brought her back from her daydreams. "Remember the one you'd kill for."

"Oh." Kathy took a bite of the apple anxious to break this sensual feeling that had engulfed her body. "Oh, God, that's good. You know if you think about it, this couldn't be that fattening because it's mostly apple."

"Nice try." Devon chuckled.

IT WAS close to six o'clock when Devon dropped Kathy at her new house. "I'll give you an hour and a half to get gorgeous."

"In that case, you'd better made it two." Kathy waved goodbye.

"Nonsense, see you at seven-thirty."

She shut the door and leaned against it. What a wonderful day. It had been perfect.

She turned on the light. This sure didn't feel like home. The place smelled musty and the walls could stand a good coat of light-colored paint. She made a mental note to get that job done in the immediate future, but tonight her mind wasn't on fixing this place up. It was on Devon and dinner -- her two favorite things.

After soaking in a hot bathtub, Kathy smoothed cream on her legs and reflected on tonight. She wanted everything to be perfect.

She went to the closet and pulled out one dress after another until she finally decided on a Royal-blue silk dress. Looking at her reflection in the full-length mirror, she fastened her belt. She brushed her hair until it shone with rich gold tones and watched as the curls fell just below her shoulders.

The doorbell rang precisely at seven-thirty. Kathy looked at her watch and smiled. She made her way to the door and opened it, then said. "I'm ready, willing and able."

Devon smiled and raised his brow before stepping into the house. "What an invitation, Luv."

Kathy stomach tightened at the gleam in his eyes. How would this night end? If the butterflies didn't quit dancing in her stomach, the night probably would end with her throwing up. She watched Devon as he turned to her. He was dressed to kill in a white dinner jacket and pink shirt.

"You look ni--. I mean beautiful tonight, birthday girl," Devon said, his eyes twinkling like diamonds.

"Are you sure it's not nice?"

"No, Luv. I'd never insult you with that nasty word again." He reached down and took her hand. "Come on, I want to show you your birthday present."

"It's here?"

He nodded and pulled her by the arm. They climbed the stairs and walked down the hall to the last room on the right. "Shut your eyes. And don't peek."

Kathy started smiling in anticipation. "I feel so silly."

"All right you can look."

Kathy slowly opened her eyes to find the room had been made into a workshop. An easel complete with canvas stood in front of her. There was a table next to the wall with tubes of paint and at the end of the room was a huge picture window.

"I don't understand." She turned to look at Devon. "Did you do all this?"

He nodded.

"Why?"

Devon chuckled. "Has senility set in at an early age . . . Your birthday . . . remember?"

Kathy frowned.

"Don't you like my present, Luv?"

"Of course, I do. I've always wanted my own studio. But what made you think of doing this?"

"When I spoke to your boss about giving you some time off. He showed me some of your work. It was quite good. I was impressed, to say the least. Old Man Wood agreed you were one of his best artists."

"Yeah, I was so good he didn't think twice about firing me."

"That had nothing to do with your talent. Anyway, I think you could be a free-lance artist and work for yourself."

"A free-lance artist? I wouldn't have any idea where to start."

"You need to begin by painting. The rest will come," Devon said with confidence. "I have some contacts that could help you."

Kathy turned to Devon. She'd dreamed of working for herself for such a long time. She wanted to hug him, but felt awkward since she'd not done so right away. He must think she was terribly ungrateful. "Thank you for your thoughtful gift."

"You're welcome."

"You know, Devon, you seem to make all my dreams come true."

He brushed his fingers along the side of her cheek. "At times, Luv, you seem like a dream to me."

CHAPTER 8

*D*evon found a quaint little Italian restaurant with beveled glass windows that stretched to cathedral ceilings, and gave a panoramic view of the Mississippi River. The maitre d' led them to a cozy, corner table where a single candle provided just the right atmosphere.

Soon their conversation shifted from one topic to another as they sipped Lancers' rosé wine. Kathy didn't know if it was the wine, her birthday, or Devon that made her mood lighthearted, but she was having a marvelous time. She loved the way Devon so intently listened when she spoke. He made her feel important and cherished and special.

"You know --" Kathy paused as the waiter placed a salad on the table, making her grimace at the rabbit-food. She ignored Devon's chuckle and finished her sentence, "--so much about me, but I don't know anything about you." *Except that you're gorgeous.* Kathy managed to keep that thought to herself. She would never forget a single detail of Devon's face, and when he stared at her like he was doing now with those big, expressive eyes, the world could be his for the asking.

"I'm lovable," he said as the corners of his mouth turned up. "What else do you need to know?"

"Be serious. Tell me a little about your family."

Devon set his wine glass down. "I'm British." He broke into a grin at her exasperated look. "All right." He held up his hand before she could complain. "I was born in a small town called Thame. I was the firstborn; my brother, Peter is twenty."

"What do your parents do for a living?"

Devon didn't answer but instead sipped his wine with deliberate slowness. "My parents manage an estate." He knew that wasn't the exact truth, but to come out and say his father was the Marquess of Edgewood and the owner of several estates made Devon sound like a stuffed shirt. And people had funny way of reacting when they found he had noble blood. They either became nervous and no longer themselves, or the women looked at him with the idea they could snag a title for themselves by marrying him. It was better that Kathy didn't know. He didn't want her attitude towards him to change.

Kathy leaned forward and propped her chin upon her hand. "What made you come to America?"

"I wanted to do something different. You know, not a chip off the old block, so to speak. I decided I wanted to study law."

The waiter approached with their dinner. Kathy grinned as he set before her a plate of spaghetti smothered with mushrooms and rich, red, tomato sauce. Devon wanted to laugh at the gleam in her eyes. He would swear she liked the food better than his present.

"Gosh, this looks great. I can't wait to taste it." Kathy

picked up the appropriate utensils and neatly twirled the pasta around her fork. She shut her eyes as she savored the first bite. Devon hadn't touched his food. Kathy's enjoyment of her food was better than a floor show. He noticed how enticing her lips looked and her words came back to him, 'Spaghetti, wine and you. I don't know which one will be the best.' At the moment, it would be no contest -- the food would win out.

She must have sensed he was staring at her because her eyelids fluttered open and she looked embarrassed. "I'm sorry you were saying something?"

God, she was a gem! "You mean you didn't hear something that important?"

"N--no. It's just that it has been so long since I've had honest to goodness food. I--I guess I got carried away. But I'm truly interested in what you were saying . . . which was?"

"You mean you missed me telling you how much I loved you?"

"You--What--Huh. You shouldn't joke about such things."

"Actually, I didn't say that," Devon admitted and the warmth of his smile echoed in his voice as he continued. "I'd make sure I had your full attention first. So needless to say, I wouldn't tell you something like that around a plate of spaghetti," he teased.

Kathy's pulse began to race. Was Devon in a roundabout way saying he loved her? She couldn't ask him again. Could she? Didn't he know she'd choose him over spaghetti any day?

"Let's have a toast before we finish dinner." He picked up his glass. "To my birthday girl. May something other than spaghetti put that gleam in your eyes."

"Devon," she said with a grin though she tried very hard not to smile as their glasses clinked together. "Now can I finish my dinner?"

A band coming through the door caught Kathy's attention, and it wasn't long before the musicians started to play soft music. She watched several couples as they danced, and soon she found herself swaying to the sound.

"May I have this dance?" Devon held out his hand.

Kathy followed him onto the dance floor where he turned and gathered her into his arms. Automatically, she placed her left hand around Devon's neck, and he held her right hand.

What a superb dancer, Kathy thought and then smiled to herself. What else should she expect from Mr. Perfect? She felt like she was floating on a cloud. Then to her surprise, Devon dropped her right hand to wrap both his arms around her. She closed her eyes and turned her face in to his neck. This was almost heaven, and she found she wanted the night to go on forever. When the music stopped, Kathy found they were both reluctant to let go of each other.

Kathy's warm breath on his neck was slowly driving him crazy. He lowered his head just a fraction and whispered in her ear. "I have a feeling we should be going."

After paying the bill, they walked outside, but instead of going to the car, Devon hailed a horse-drawn carriage. The highly-polished carriage gleamed as the brass-spoked wheels came to a stop.

"What are you doing?"

"We're going on a tour of New Orleans, Ma'am."

Kathy laughed at Devon mocking a Southern drawl. She stepped up into the sleek, black carriage and sat upon the red velvet cushions. She felt just like a Princess with Prince Charming beside her.

A black man sitting high on his perched seat turned and tipped his hat to them. "Where to, Sir?"

"We'd like a tour of the French Quarter at a slow pace, please," Devon instructed.

"Yes, Sir. Giddy up, Sally," the driver called to his horse.

The carriage moved smoothly as the horse's hoofs clip-clopped on the pavement. New Orleans put on a different face at night. The lights glittered. And the sidewalks filled with people: some walking, some dancing, some trying to earn a living by playing music. She could hear Cajun and jazz music as they rode past several open lounge doors. Even the smell of gumbo and crayfish managed to escape the kitchens and linger in the streets.

"This is a first for me," Kathy told Devon. "I moved to New Orleans about eight years ago, and though I've strolled through the French Quarter many times, I've never taken a tour. I feel like a tourist." She smiled before adding, "I guess tonight I am."

"In that case, I'm glad I'm the one to show you a very special city."

Kathy listened as the driver told them that most of the buildings had been built on cotton bails. That's why the floors in some of the structures were uneven. Kathy was thoroughly enjoying herself, but she had to stifle another yawn. She didn't want Devon to think she was bored, but between the wine and lack of sleep, she could feel her eyelids growing heavier by the minute.

Devon twisted and reached in his pocket, pulling out a long, silver box, which he handed to her.

Instantly, she became alert. "What's this?"

"Since you were not impressed by my other gift," he said with a subtle look of amusement on his face. "I thought I'd give you another."

"But I liked your first present," Kathy protested. "I was just merely shocked that you knew something about my painting. Here." She tried to hand him back his gift. "You've done more than enough."

Instead of taking the gift back, Devon put his right arm around her completely ignoring her request. He studied her intently before he spoke. "Perhaps, you deserve two presents."

His eyes darkened with tenderness, and for Kathy, the busy sidewalks became a murmur in the background. Finally, she pulled her gaze away from him. "You shouldn't have, Devon." She laughed, her fingers fumbling with the paper. "But since you did." She tore away the last shreds of tissue opened the long black box. A soft gasp escaped her lips as a warm glow flowed through her body.

A fine linked chain of 18 Karat gold gleamed up at her from its velvet bed. And suspended at the end of the chain was a skillfully-crafted, old-fashioned key with a small ruby encrusted at the top.

"It's beautiful," Kathy breathed, too stunned to cry and too numb to laugh. This wasn't some cheap trinket, but an expensive gold masterpiece.

The lashes that shadowed her cheeks flew up. "Thank you. But why a key?"

Devon took the necklace out of the box and fastened it around Kathy's neck. "It's the key that unlocks my heart."

She jerked her head up and looked into his whisky-brown eyes, and once again became mesmerized by their softness. Had she heard him correctly, or had she merely heard what she wanted to hear? "But will my key work?"

Kathy whispered, afraid of breaking the spell. Then with trembling fingers, she reached up and touched his smooth cheek. His warm flesh felt good as she slid her fingers to the back of his head.

She had her answer as Devon's mouth covered hers. Tender, yet insistent lips caressed her mouth. She reached up and grasped his lapel with her other hand like a drowning victim fighting for his life and sanity. She was stunned by his urgency. And he was demanding a response from her. Which she intended to give him.

He had ignited in her a hunger she had thought died a long time ago. Isn't this what she wanted? What she'd dreamed of for so long?

Many sensations raced through her body, and she found Devon's touch made her yearn for something more. And to her surprise, she heard bells, or was it a loud crash?

The driver cleared his throat, trying to gain their attention before speaking. "Sorry to break this up folks, but I fear that thunder means we're in for a good dousing. Better head back."

Lightening flashed again in the distance as Devon lifted his head and turned to the driver. "It does appear as if we might experience a bit of trouble."

Kathy rested her head on Devon's shoulder. So it hadn't been bells . . . only thunder. Damn! And she had thought it had been a sign they might be a good match. She couldn't go through another bad relationship. Tonight she'd go merely on her gut feelings. Take one thing at a time. And pray.

Just as the restaurant came into sight, a mist began to fall. Lightly at first, but by the time Devon paid the driver it had turned into a steady rain.

"Head for the car!" Devon grabbed Kathy's elbow

firmly and together they ran. He pressed the remote door locks and they both scooted inside the Jag.

"I bet you never thought tonight included a bath?" Devon reached under the seat and produced a small hand towel. Being the gentleman he was, he handed it to her first. When she was through, he dried his own arms.

"When I'm with you there's always a surprise or two," Kathy admitted.

"Just as long as I'm not boring you," he said before backing the car out of the parking lot. "I'm going to stop by my place and find some dry clothes."

"Good. Then I can see where you live."

WHEN THEY ARRIVED at Devon's town house, the rain had not let up in the least. If anything it was coming down harder.

"Stay here and I'll bring back an umbrella for you."

"It's only a short distance," Kathy protested. "Besides, the damage is already done. I can make it."

"Nonsense. There's no need in both of us getting soaked again."

Kathy watched as he ran to the door and fumbled to get the key in the lock. Funny, she had imagined Devon living in a big house instead of an apartment. Perhaps, the fact that he was single had a great deal to do with his living arrangements.

Soon Devon appeared with an umbrella. He helped her out of the car, but before they could get to the house a gust of wind snatched the umbrella from Devon's hand, leaving them no choice, but to duck their heads and run the rest of the way through the pouring rain.

Kathy stood in the foyer, dripping water on Devon's black-and-white tile floor. She pushed some wet hair from her face and looked down at her once-silky dress that now clung to every curve she had, and a few she wished would go away.

"I don't want to get on your carpet like this." She held out her arms.

"Here." Devon handed her a rose-colored towel. "I grabbed a few towels before I went out to get you."

Kathy patted her arms and legs, then dried her feet. She started laughing at herself. Instead of being sexy, she now looked like a drowned cat. "I guess I look kind of rough?"

"On the contrary." He laughed. "I like the cling on that dress." He winked.

Kathy felt her whole body turn red as she tugged at the wet material. "Perhaps, I should take it off?"

"I like that idea even better."

"I--I mean change into something else."

"I know what you mean." He finally admitted before draping a towel around his neck. "Go down the hall and take the first door on the right. My robe is behind the door. While you change, I'll light a fire to take the chill from our bones."

It was no small job removing a pair of soaking wet panty hose. After she finally managed to peel them off without breaking her neck, she removed the dress followed by her bra.

Kathy looked at herself in the mirror. What was she thinking? It was true she had lost a lot of weight, but look at this body. First, her breasts were too big, she tried to put her hands underneath each to hoist them higher. No use. Her critical eyes traveled a little further. There was the scar where she had her appendix removed. Her hands slid down to her waist where she pinched an inch . . . hell, she could grab a whole hand full. "It's hopeless," she groaned. "And look at these stretch marks!" Devon probably had been to bed with model-perfect women. He would take one look at her body and compare her to the other beauties that he'd dated. As she rolled her eyes, she saw the key dangling between her breasts and smiled. Maybe he did care . . . Just a little. She looked up to heaven and whispered, "Please God, don't let him be disappointed."

Kathy had to roll the sleeves up on his black velour robe. She felt as if Devon was caressing her skin as she wrapped the bathrobe around her and tied it at the waist. His scent was all over the garment and she could feel her heart beat just a little faster with anticipation. She blew her hair dry and went back to the living room.

ORANGE FLAMES LEAPED over the gas logs and a multitude of candles flickered along the mantel and around the room.

Devon stood in front of the fire with his arm propped casually on the wooden mantel over the fireplace. Soft music played in the background, and Kathy wondered what Devon was thinking as he stared into the flames. When she cleared her throat, he turned and smiled.

"Come, stand by the fire. Here's a little brandy to warm you." He handed her a snifter filled with dark amber-colored liquid. "I heard on the radio that there is a bad storm off the coast producing this downpour. They are advising people to stay off the roads."

Kathy saw beads of moisture on Devon's forehead, and

throwing caution to the wind, she picked up a corner of the burgundy towel and wiped his brow. "Then it appears . . . I'll have to stay here." She whispered huskily then grinned.

"Appears so." He smiled, leaned down and brushed her lips. "I better get out of these wet clothes," he said before leaving.

Kathy moved over to the sliding glass door that led to a screened porch. She opened the door slightly so she could hear the rain. Propping her shoulder on the door jam, she sipped the brandy and listened to the soft music enhanced by the rain drops. God, this was heaven!

Swirling the brandy around her glass, she yawned. Again her sleepless night was taking its toll. Now after propositioning Devon, *it would be just like her to fall asleep* and miss whatever the night might hold. She shivered at a delicious thought as a breeze blew her hair around her face. She reached up and tucked the stray strand of hair behind her ear.

"Do you like the sound of rain, Luv?" Devon whispered into her hair as his arms came around her.

"Mmmm. It's so relaxing," she murmured.

"Did the brandy warm you?"

"Not as much as you do," Kathy admitted. It must be the liquor making her talk so bold. Devon was going to think she was the most forward female . . . the most desperate woman he'd ever met. *B--But . . . it has been so long!* She wanted to shout. "D--Devon I don't think I've ever felt like this before." She turned and looked into his dark eyes.

"How is that?"

"I'm not sure."

"Dance with me." Devon removed the glass from her

hand his fingers brushing hers before he sat the snifter on the mantel. Kathy immediately noticed he had on blue jeans and he hadn't bothered to button his white shirt. Devon's black chest hairs peeked from beneath his shirt and looked all so inviting on his olive skin.

She was hauled forward into arms of steel and she remembered seeing a flicker of orange and red flames as she shut her eyes and laid her head on Devon's shoulder. In the distance, the radio announced before playing the next song. "This is a night for lovers."

Kathy had to agree. The sound of the raindrops dancing on the roof, and the breeze that sneaked through the door, and of course, the pounding of Kathy's heart were the only sounds that she was conscious of; that is, until the music changed to "Crying." Just like in the movie "Dirty Dancing." It was the last straw for Kathy. She wanted Devon no matter what the cost.

He lowered his head and kissed her long and slow, their sensual bodies rubbing together and never missing a beat of the music. When Devon's mouth left hers, he kissed her chin and Kathy let her head fall backwards as Devon trailed kisses down her throat. "I want you, Kathy," he murmured against her skin.

Slowly, she opened her dream-filled eyes. "I want you, too," she whispered.

He kissed the tip of her nose. "Are you sure?" he asked, giving her a chance to change her mind.

She stared at him not bothering to answer. Instead she ran her hands under his shirt and placed soft kisses on his chest, feeling his firm muscles grow taut by her touch. Once again her eyes met his. "Yes, I'm sure."

The words were barely torn from her throat before his mouth swept down on hers. Evidently, all his other kisses had been mild because now her mouth throbbed with the crush of his lips. His hold tightened around her as if he were afraid she'd slip away. Her footsteps faltered and she thought she'd faint from dizziness, but as soon as she stumbled, Devon loosened his grip and his hand drifted across her back in soothing strokes. Once again they picked up the rhythm of the music.

He tenderly urged her lips apart so his tongue could slide between them. She marveled at the multitude of rapid emotions that ran through her as his tongue explored the recesses of her mouth.

Kathy longed to tell Devon how much she loved him, but she was afraid she would scare him off.

"I think you have on too many clothes, Luv," he murmured on her lips. With dexterous fingers, he slowly untied her robe and let it fall open. Kathy squeezed her eyes shut afraid to look at the laughter in his eyes, but to her amazement, she heard no laughter. She jumped when he lifted his hand to cup her breast. "Beautiful," he murmured as he rubbed his thumb across her smooth skin.

She opened her eyes and heat engulfed her body as Devon stared at her. He wasn't appalled. He thought she was beautiful!

Devon sensed Kathy was shy and knew he needed to move slowly. However, when she reached up and slid his shirt off, the tremors that shook him almost made him forget his vow. Go slow, he reminded himself, go slow.

Brushing her ear with feather-light caress, he kissed her soft earlobe and marveled at how she smelled of honeysuckle. He shut his eyes and pictured the flowers clinging to a gray fence in a spring meadow when he was a boy. It had been his favorite smell. She melted her body into his and again they were moving with the music -- always the music

-- mindless of the tune. "You know, Kathy, I never intended to feel anything for you," Devon murmured against her skin. "I wanted to fulfill a last request and get on with my life." Again he tightened his hold and Kathy found she was holding her breath waiting to see what else he would say. "And then you walked into my office, and instead of seeing your good fortune, you wanted nothing to do with me."

He placed his hand under her chin and tilted it up. "I think that was the day you unknowingly changed my life."

"I hope it was for the good."

"Yes." He smiled. "It was for the good."

Kathy felt protected as she returned his smile. His hand slid back to her neck and his fingers began to stroke soft skin.

His lips descended to hers and she lifted her chin slightly. At first, he brushed her lips and pressed her breast into his chest. He liked the feel of her satin-flesh next to his. His tongue lightly flicked across her lips until she parted them in response. The passion deep in her eyes told Devon she was ready for his love-making. It was the only invitation he needed as his tongue plunged into her mouth.

A deep wild hunger stirred Kathy, leaving her clinging to Devon. His hands slid down her back at a torturous pace where he pressed her pelvis next to him. That's when Kathy felt the rough material and realized Devon still had on his jeans.

Breaking away from those wonderful lips was difficult, but pressing her hands against his chest, she pulled back.

Kathy could see the puzzlement in his eyes before he asked. "What's wrong?"

She merely smiled and seductively dropped her gaze inch by inch all the way down his chest . . . lower and lower. Devon felt like he'd been burned every place her eyes touched. As her fingers slid just inside his jeans, she popped the snap and grasped the zipper. Devon jumped and drew in his breath. "I think we can do without these," she said softly. He couldn't agree more. She dipped her head and ever so slowly, she inched the zipper down while running her tongue lightly across his chest.

"Oh, God," Devon groaned aloud. If she didn't hurry up and remove his jeans he was going to tear them off and bury himself inside her. *God, what sweet torture.* As she shoved his jeans down, her kisses lowered to his stomach, and her tongue circled his naval. Shuddering, he managed to rasp out, "Don't."

Kicking his jeans and undershorts aside, he pulled her quickly against his now nude body. He wanted to feel every inch of her against him.

Confused Kathy asked, "Why?"

"Because." Devon nuzzled her neck as he finished slipping off her robe. Throwing, it down in front of the fireplace, he said honestly, "I'm about to explode, Luv . . . much more of that and I would have."

"Then you like what I do to you?" Kathy asked. His lips were within an inch of hers begging to be explored. Her nipples had turned hard and throbbed for his touch. It should be a sin for anything to feel this wonderful.

"I don't ever remember anybody setting me on fire like you have," he growled.

A gust of wet air slipped in the sliding glass doors and wafted across their bodies. Kathy shivered. "I think the storm grows worse." Just as Kathy spoke lightening struck and the power flickered once, twice then went out, ending their romantic music.

Devon chuckled, "Since the storm took out our entertainment . . . I guess we'll have to make our own." He wrapped his fingers in her silky hair and pulled her head back so he could claim her breast.

His tongue circled and sucked, caressing her rosy-brown nipples. Kathy's vision blurred as she ran her hands through his black hair. When she thought she could take no more, he switched to the other breast and before she realized what he was doing his fingers began stroking, and finally settling in the warmth between her legs.

Kathy trembled and Devon responded. He sucked just a little harder as his fingers moved with a rhythm all their own. When he took the hard bud between his teeth, he heard Kathy moan.

"Devon," Kathy whimpered. "Please, I need you now."

He lowered her to the floor and immediately his lips began their assault. Kathy had slept with one other man, but it had never been anything like this. She'd never felt all the things she did now. Boldly touching her tongue to his, the low growl of pleasure in the back of his throat told her she pleased him.

Absentmindedly, she moved her hands up Devon's back as their tongues tangled together wildly. Every time he shifted, Kathy felt a cool breeze blowing over them. Both their bodies were damp and hot and demanding. Was it raining harder or was that the blood roaring in her ears?

Devon lifted his head and looked at her dazed expression and swollen lips. She couldn't hide the passion in her eyes nor the love, and now Devon wanted her more than ever. Rubbing his arousal against her warmth, the unbearable pressure finally became too much. He lifted her hips and with a full-force need to relieve his agony, he plunged deeply.

Katherine's eyes flew open. He was so deep in her body she felt her pause race out of control. Her heart thumped wildly against her ribs and when she started to follow his rhythm, a motion as old as time. She found her hands sliding up his arms, as uncontrollable excitement shook her body, making her cry out her love for Devon.

Devon, knowing he had pleased her, found his own fulfillment. Still holding Kathy, he rolled to his side, and waited for his breathing to once again become normal while he pondered these new found feelings for the woman in his arms. Her slow steady breathing told him she had fallen asleep.

Looking up to heaven, he saw Catherine Dubois. And she was smiling down at him.

Yes, somehow he knew . . . Catherine had planned this all along.

CHAPTER 9

"*D*evon, darling." A lush brunette bent over and kissed Devon on the cheek. "I didn't know you were coming to the club today."

Kathy would never know what Devon was about to say. He merely released her hand and turned to the pretty, perfectly-shaped woman whom Kathy already knew she couldn't stand.

"Whitney," Devon greeted. "You look fetching today."

Kathy noticed what he didn't say, and she couldn't help but smile as she itched to say . . . *didn't you mean nice?* And wouldn't you know the gorgeous woman even had a beautiful name.

"I thought you had work to do." Whitney looked at Kathy for the first time.

Kathy stiffened. Somehow she'd forgotten she was Devon's client and nothing more than work for him. For a moment, she had thought that Devon liked her just a little. Evidently, she had been wrong, just like she usually was when it came to men.

"This is Katherine Taylor. And Kathy . . ." He turned

and when his eyes met hers, she could see a hint of embarrassment in their depths. " . . . I'd like you to meet Whitney, a friend of mine."

"It's nice to meet you." Kathy felt the polite words tumble from her mouth -- though it was far from how she felt -- as she held out her hand.

The woman nodded then dismissed Kathy as if she wasn't worthy of being a threat to her.

Kathy put her hand back in her lap. The snub made her feel small, but somewhere her inner strength kicked in, and she silently vowed that someday this woman would look at her differently.

"I'll run along and leave you to your business stuff," Whitney said. "See you about seven. By the way, sweetheart, I'm cooking your favorite tonight."

Sweetheart? Kathy wanted to puke. Yet she couldn't figure out why she was so upset. Of course, he'd be dating. And of course, it would be someone pretty -- even though Whitney sounded like a first class air-head. But when you're pretty, who needs brains? Was Devon drawn to that type of woman? Did he love her?

"It's a shame you have to work on Saturdays. This should be our day to relax and enjoy," Whitney purred, making her point that they usually did just that.

"Didn't you say you were leaving?"

Whitney stiffened at Devon's sharp words. "I'll see you tonight, darling."

An uncomfortable silence lingered after she left. Kathy sipped her tea, which she was having a hard time choking down as her anger rose. What was he thinking? That poor, pitiful Kathy had her feelings hurt . . . well to hell with him. She couldn't handle his pity. Pity was not what she wanted, and she wasn't some mealy-mouthed snit who he'd walk over.

"Kath -- I . . ."

"Don't pity me!" She pushed back her chair and stood, staring icily at Devon. She said, in as level a voice as she could manage, "Save it! Your friend was right. It's a shame you have to work on Saturday. Evidently, this is the day you usually spend with *her*," Kathy snapped, not really caring that they were drawing an audience. "Well, Mr. York, you're now off the job. And since you have been working, please pay the check out of *my* account. I do believe you have control of *my* money." She swung around just as he reached out to grab her arm and fled before he could pay the waiter and catch her.

When she reached the car, she searched frantically for her car keys. "Why did I carry such a big purse?" Kathy swore, knowing she was losing precious minutes. Her fingers fumbled over everything except the damn keys. She had to leave here before he came after her, that is, if he did come. Devon more than likely was glad to be rid of her. Tears started to trickle down her cheeks. Why had she begun to care about a man she could never have? She knew he would only break her heart. Her fingers finally brushed the metal, and with a relieved sigh, she pulled out the key and slipped it into the lock.

A hand slid down her arm and stopped her from opening the door. She jumped. But the heat from his body calmed her as she breathed in his woodsy scent. It was Devon. His breath felt warm on her neck as he moved his hands to her shoulders and turned her around as he murmured. "I'm sorry, Luv. I wouldn't have hurt you for anything."

She refused to look at him. "What made you think I

was hurt? You should listen to your girlfriend and spend Saturdays with her." Kathy stared at the button on his shirt. "We're nothing more than a mere business arrangement."

He placed his hand under her chin and tilted it upward. With the back of his finger he wiped the tears from her cheeks while he kept her body firmly pressed next to his. "Then why do you cry?" he whispered.

Captured by his rich brown eyes, she wanted to kiss the playboy who held her so intimately . . . and in the worst way. But it would never do. No never. "I always cry after lunch. Especially when I have to eat tuna."

Devon laughed and folded her in his arms, kissing the top of her head. "Do you know, Kathy, I never laughed much until you came into my life."

She noticed he'd slipped and used her nickname, and she couldn't help her smile. Well, it was something. Not a declaration of love, but something that seemed to make her special to him. And God, it felt good to be wrapped in his embrace, and she was thankful he could get his arms around her.

Devon pulled back. "You are not just a job, Luv. To be truthful, I don't know what you are to me, but we're bound together for the next six months. And I'm looking forward to being friends. I'll pick you up Monday at six for our exercise. Be sure to wear your tights."

"Yeah, sure." Kathy snickered. "Now that will make you laugh. Hell, you'll probably crack your ribs laughing so hard."

"One day, Luv, you're not going to have your weight to make jokes about." He cocked his head to the side. "Do you suppose I'll like you as much then?"

Friends, Kathy sighed as she slid into her car and rolled down the window. "I guess, we'll just have to see."

THIS SURE HAS BEEN a strange day, Kathy thought as she pulled into the driveway of her apartment.

She stuck her head into the doorway and yelled. "Tina. Come see my car."

Tina's eyes grew wide in surprise. "It's new!"

"Sure is. Can you believe I have a car that hasn't been owned by at least two other people?"

"I've never had a new car." Tina ran her hand over the vehicle. "Did Prince Charming help you pick it out?"

"Yes, he did. And afterwards we went to the Country Club for lunch."

"He took *you* to the Country Club?" Tina asked. Her amazement showed clearly in the depths of her eyes.

Kathy nodded.

"Why?"

Kathy looked directly at Tina and wondered why she asked such a stupid question. "I told you we went for lunch. Why do you find that so hard to believe?"

Tina shrugged her shoulders. "What's in this for him?"

"Perhaps he likes me and is just being friendly. After all, he was friends with Aunt Catherine." Kathy opened the car door and got out her purse. Why did Tina have to spoil a good day?

"Are you sure there isn't a clause in her will that says if you meet your goal, Devon will be generously rewarded?" Tina asked. "That would explain why he is determined to help you lose weight."

"Of course not!" Kathy shook her head, denying the

accusation. "You always look on the dark side of things. You're such a pessimist," she spat as she swept passed Tina.

"How about a realist," Tina called to her sister's back. Kathy went to her room and threw her keys on the dresser before sitting on the bed to remove her shoes. Tina was just jealous. Devon couldn't be that devious. He had just been polite. Yet -- hadn't she asked him the same question that Tina had just brought up? Kathy shook her head, refusing to let her thoughts wander down that path.

Later that night as she slept, Devon crept into her dreams. Again she felt his arms around her and the fragrance of British Sterling linger ever so lightly in the air. He tilted her chin up and lowered his lips to hers. She caught her breath in anticipation as he drew close. She knew this was what she wanted, but just as he was about to kiss her, he started to laugh. Her eyelids flew open. The spell was broken. Startled, she could only stare as he said, "It was for the money, Kathy . . . merely the money."

A strangled cry tore from her throat, and she sat straight up in bed. "Damn you, Tina, for putting doubts in my mind. Why couldn't you leave well enough alone? I will not believe it," Kathy stammered in a voice that seemed like a buzz in her ears. Her head began to throb. Aunt Catherine wouldn't have liked Devon if he were devious. She just wouldn't have.

MONDAY SEEMED to drag by as Kathy kept her mind on her various drawings. She had just finished a single red rose topping it off with glistening rain drops. Proud of her work, she could very well write the saying for this card.

"Roses are red and violets are blue. I hope one day you'll love me, too."

Damn she needed to get her head out of the clouds and off Devon.

THE WEEKEND HAD GONE by in a blur. Even though Devon had been busy, he had thought of Kathy more than once during the day. He remembered her hurt expression when she ran out of the restaurant, if it had been any other woman he would have let her go, but instead he ran after her not wanting Kathy to be upset. The urge to protect her was strong in him. In many ways, she reminded him of himself. He'd not found a lady who had held his interest in a long time, but something about this one drew him like a moth to a flame.

His date with Whitney had been the usual dull conversation and afterward they had made love, which he'd found quite satisfying. But it hadn't been Whitney's face Devon saw, and that fact had shaken him more than he cared to admit. Suddenly, his life felt cold. Empty. But now wasn't the time to be seriously involved with anyone. He had big plans for his future, and he mustn't get sidetracked except for this one little adventure with Kathy. But that would only be six months of his time then it would be over.

Arriving at Kathy's apartment precisely at six, he knocked and waited.

"Come in." Tina pulled open the door and motioned with her hand for Devon to enter. "Kathy's still trying to squeeze into her tights. Can I get you something to drink? You might have to wait awhile." Tina laughed at her little joke.

"No thanks. I'll just stay here." Devon found it amazing how vastly different the two sisters were. Tina had a coldness about her he didn't quite care for.

"I'm ready, and you better not laugh," Kathy called just before she walked out wearing pink tights and a big tee shirt with the words *So much to love* written across the front.

As hard as he tried not to laugh, it was impossible. "I'm sorry, Luv. I'm not laughing at your tights, but that bloody shirt."

"Yeah, sure." She punched him affectionately in the ribs as she walked past him. "See you later, Tina."

"You two have fun. Take your key, Kathy. I've got a date and won't be in until late."

To say Kathy was a little self-conscious when she entered the club would have been putting it mildly. A pretty young girl greeted them when they walked in.

"Nancy." Devon spoke to her, and Kathy couldn't help wondering if he had dated her, too. "I'd like to start my friend on an exercise program. Can you handle the job?"

"No problem, Devon. Just leave her with me." Her eyes glowed with admiration as she talked to him. "I believe you know your way around."

No wonder he wasn't conceited, Kathy thought. He seemed to conquer women like a Roman solider.

After he left, Nancy turned to her. "What's your name?"

"Kathy."

"It's a pleasure to meet a friend of Devon's. You were probably the envy of every woman in here when you walked in with him. He's considered a catch, but I guess you know that," she spoke eagerly. "Now tell me what exercises are you doing, so I know where to start."

"To be truthful —" Kathy paused, and her embarrassment showed, " -- none. I'm afraid I am one of those people who had good attentions, but never seem to get around to the actual deed."

"I know what you mean." Nancy laughed. "Let's start off slow so you don't get sore." She grabbed her clipboard and motioned to Kathy. "Follow me."

Nancy led her over to the exercise bikes. "I want you to start by riding five miles," she said as Kathy took her seat. "I'll be back in a few minutes to check on you."

"If I ride five miles there probably won't be anything left to check," Kathy mumbled as she began to pedal. Surprisingly, it wasn't hard at all. She watched her feet going round and round, feeling very superior that she had conquered the machine. When she looked around the room for Devon, she spied him with his back to her talking to someone who Kathy couldn't see. An aquamarine towel draped around his neck made his hair look just that much darker. He stood casually and his muscular legs were well displayed. Unfortunately, everything about Devon was perfect . . . too perfect. She didn't think she'd ever get tired of staring at his darkly tanned body. What a contrast they were: perfect and not so perfect.

Devon turned as if he felt her staring at him and started her way. Kathy looked past him to see that it had been Whitney he'd been talking to. Kathy's stomach muscles tightened, and it wasn't from the exercise. She knew she needed to control her lusting reactions to the man. There wasn't a chance in hell she could hold his attention when there were so many beautiful women around. He and Whitney had probably been planning their upcoming date, she thought, then wondered if Whitney knew how lucky she was.

Devon now stood in front of her smiling. "How are you doing?"

"This is much easier than I thought," Kathy boasted as she tried to pedal faster to impress him.

Devon walked around and looked down at the gauges on the bike and frowned. "I guess it is since you don't have any tension on the thing." He reached over and punched a couple of buttons. Automatically, her rhythm went from Speedy Gonzales to a snail's pace.

"What did you do that for?" Kathy gasped while her feet barely turned the pedals.

"The more tension you have on the bike, the more calories you burn. The more calories you burn, the faster you lose weight. After all, that's why we're here."

Kathy could already feel the pull on her legs. "You're the boss," she grudgingly acknowledged. *And if I die on this thing, you'll be the one to carry me out. Think about that, pretty boy!*

"Good girl." He patted her shoulder then moved to the other side of the room.

Great, she thought. Now he's patting me like one would a pet.

KATHY SPENT the next hour with various exercises, and finally her instructor suggested the sauna and a shower. Nancy had informed her that Devon was swimming laps.

Kathy opened the sauna door. White steam poured out as she walked into the room. Peering through the mist, she couldn't see anyone, so she picked a corner and sat down, drawing her knees up and wrapping her arms around them.

A few minutes later, the door opened and another woman entered and moved to the other side. When she drew closer, Kathy could see it was Whitney.

"Kathy," Whitney acknowledged her presence. "How do you like our little club?"

"It's not bad," Kathy commented nonchalantly. Then she decided she should be cordial. "Have you been a member long?"

"About three years. Devon talked me into joining so we could do more things together. He's a very considerate man."

"I haven't known him long, but he does seem thoughtful," Kathy agreed.

"He'd pick up any stray and try to take care of it. I guess that's why I love him."

Whitney's words cut deep, but before Kathy could say anything, Nancy stuck her head into the room and said, "Time's up, Kathy."

As she stepped out of the sauna Whitney said, "It's been a pleasure chatting with you."

Kathy turned to look at her. "Wasn't it though." She wanted to add the word *bitch*, but she was, after all, at the country club.

ON THE DRIVE HOME, Kathy remained quiet, thinking of Whitney. She definitely seemed to love Devon, and Kathy couldn't blame her. Perhaps, she would stop all these silly notions about him and maybe they could be just friends.

When they arrived at her apartment Devon

commented. "You're mighty quiet, Luv. Are you tired?"

"A little," she murmured. "Thank you for taking me with you. Would you like to come in and have a snack and a drink?"

"I believe I would."

Kathy unlocked the door and slung her purse, which was her usual custom, but this time she missed the chair and the contents scattered out. "Damn!"

"Here I'll help you." Devon was quick to get on his knees and assist. "And just what is this?" He held up a package of malted milk balls.

"My emergency boost." Kathy's eyes grew wide with guilt. "I never know when my blood sugar will take a plunge," she joked but found he wasn't laughing.

He eyed her suspiciously before standing up and pulling her to her feet. "Come on."

"Where are we going?"

He didn't brother to answer but pulled her behind him until they reached the kitchen. "Where's the light?"

Kathy flipped the switch on and watched as he went over and opened the refrigerator door. He saw a blueberry pie, a chocolate pie, a coconut cake, some country-style steak and half a pizza!

"Christ, Kathy!" Devon slammed the door, jarring its contents. Turning, he grabbed her by the shoulders. He was so angry he felt like shaking her. Here he was trying to help her, and she was hoarding enough food for an army battalion.

"All the exercise in the world will not help if you continue to eat like this! You must watch what you eat, and of course, eat less." His fingers tightened on her arm. "Why did you cook all this? I thought we had an agreement."

She had never seen him so angry. His brown eyes held a look she didn't care for. "I didn't cook it." She shrugged out of his grip. "Tina did. She's a very good cook."

"I bet she is," he snapped. "And I bet Tina just loves to cook even more since you started on your diet. Doesn't she?"

"Well . . . yes, but I eat small portions," Kathy admitted, then added, "Tina said it wouldn't hurt."

"And if Tina told you to jump off a cliff -- I'd bet you'd do that, too. Somehow, I don't feel she has your best interest at heart," he said, and each word rang with anger. "She doesn't want to see you succeed."

"How can you say that? She's my sister and wouldn't do anything to harm me."

He leaned against the beige countertop and folded his arms across his chest. "Deliberate hurt . . . probably not. But keeping you fat and under her thumb so she can be the beautiful sister who gets all the attention, I wouldn't put that past her." He paused. "Do you want that?"

"No." Kathy could only stand in front of him looking miserable. Could Tina really be that malicious? She was always putting her down.

"Well neither do I. You are going to reach your goal if I personally have to feed you. Then, if you don't like the way you are, you can go back to being as fat as a pig."

Kathy's golden eyes shot sparks in his direction. "So that's the way you see me -- a pig?"

Devon immediately regretted his choice of words. "No, I was just angry."

"What's in this for you Devon?" she blurted out. "Are you not paid the same whether I lose weight or not?" This time she was the one to reach out and grab his arm. "Why do you want to concern yourself with a fat little pig?"

Her warm hand burned his skin. He stared at her, loving the gold specks in the center of her eyes. Mesmerized, he took her hand in his, caressing it softly with his thumb. "Because I know what it's like to be put down constantly and never have any confidence in oneself. It can destroy you, Luv."

"You?" Somehow she found it hard to believe that Mr. Perfect had ever had any problems. But she sensed this near confession of his had been hard.

"That's right. Until I met your aunt and she challenged me to be the best I could be. She was there when I needed her, and I'll be here when you need me."

"So you're doing this because of my aunt?" Knowing that's not what she wanted to hear, she couldn't help asking the questions that always haunted her.

"Partially." He shrugged. Watching her confusion, he felt the need to touch her and reached over and ran his thumb along her jawline. Her smooth ivory skin and gold-flecked eyes had begun to haunt his dreams. "I'm doing this because I care."

Kathy raised her brow in doubt. "For me?" Devon's touch became intimate as his thumb moved seductively back along her jaw.

"Yes, for you. Why do you find that so hard to believe?"

"Because I'm fat."

He jerked his hand back as if she'd burnt him with her words. He thought for a moment, running both his hands though his hair. When he looked back to her, his eyes held a different light in them. "I like you, Katherine, especially your personality. When I look at you, I see a beautiful person. True, I want you to lose weight, but it still will not change the person I've come to know."

"What about Whitney?" Kathy asked, gently. "She told me tonight she loved you."

"I do date several women, but I don't love any of them. I'm not sure I've ever loved anyone." His voice grew tender as he slipped his hand under her hair to the back of her neck, pulling her a little closer. "Have you ever loved, Kathy?"

"Y--Yes." His fingers produced shivers of delight up and down her spine, but she managed to squeak out. "O--Or at least I thought I had until he ran off with someone else."

"I'm sorry, Luv," Devon murmured. "If I could erase the hurt I would."

"W--would you?" Her nervousness finally sounded in her voice.

He nodded, knowing he felt something for her, but love? That Devon still wasn't sure of. One thing he did know was that he wanted to kiss her. Not because she was fat. Not because he felt sorry for her, but because of the person she was inside. The one he'd come to adore.

She jumped when his other hand moved to her back and in one swift movement pulled her against his body. He tilted her face up toward him and smiled a lazy smile before he closed his eyes and lowered his head.

Kathy's heart leapt in her throat. He was going to kiss her just like in her dream. How long had it been since she'd been kissed by a man? Would she remember what to do? Would she kiss as well as Whitney? Kathy didn't have time to answer any of those questions before his lips brushed hers ever so lightly.

"Should I have asked permission to kiss you, my love?" Devon asked in a voice full of emotion. Yet, he didn't wait for the answer as his arms imprisoned her.

He felt tenderness when his lips took hers in a fierce kiss. Her arms wrapped around his neck and he deepened his kiss, his hungry lips grew persuasive and soon she parted hers and his tongue slid between them. He felt her respond and heard her soft moan. Just as his senses began to explode, she pressed her body into his.

Kathy's desire was now working in overdrive. Never had she been kissed like this. She had thought maybe she was frigid and incapable of loving. But mounting desire ran rapid over her body like a short circuit. And when he began to French-kiss her, she marveled at her new height of passion. She felt his hard thigh muscles against her legs. Devon tasted good, felt good, looked good, and God, help her not to drag him straight to the bedroom.

He raised his head and stared down at her passion-filled eyes. "I believe I've gotten off the subject."

"I don't mind."

"I can see that." He smiled before releasing her and moving to the other side of the kitchen. He grew quiet for a few minutes before he spoke. "I think I need to get you away from here. Then maybe your diet will work."

"Where? I do have to work you know." She sensed he didn't want to discuss the kiss. Perhaps, he already regretted his actions.

"If you make your goal, you'll never have to work again," he gently reminded her. "I've a place in mind where people go to get in shape. I'll make all the arrangements. I think Weatherford is just the place for you."

"You're sending me to a fat farm?"

His devilish smile proved he was pleased with himself. He completely ignored her statement as he continued. "The more I think about it the better I like the idea. Weatherford is just what you need."

CHAPTER 10

*K*athy couldn't remember when she had slept so well. Opening her eyes, everything came flooding back. She was still in Devon's bed, so yesterday could not have been a dream.

Sunlight bathed the room in soft yellow; therefore, she knew it must be midmorning. She didn't remember Devon slipping out of bed, but she did recall him pulling her close in the early hours of morning. It had been pure heaven, having his warm body next to hers. So where was he? And more important how did he feel this morning? It was Sunday so she knew he didn't have to work. Perhaps he was having second thoughts?

She frowned and threw back the covers as doubts crept through her head. Then she remembered Devon carrying her in this room last night. He'd been so tender . . . so loving.

As her feet hit the floor, she realized the bathrobe was still in the living room and there wasn't anything else to put on. Her eyes scanned the room. The closet. There was bound to be something in there. She opened the door and looked at the dozens of shirts and slacks hanging neatly in a row, sorted by colors. Ah, a clue to his personality. He was neat, and unfortunately, she was the opposite. Taking out a blue shirt, she slipped it on and quickly buttoned the garment as she walked into the bathroom. She rinsed her mouth out and brushed her hair to remove the tangles before finding Devon. She didn't want to look like a witch first thing in the morning.

Now to find Devon. Leaving the room, she moved down the hall and through the living room blushing at the crumpled bathrobe -- the evidence -- that still laid in the middle of the floor.

From the kitchen, she heard a clang and a "bloody hell."

She peeked around the corner and found Devon wiping the cabinets where he'd evidently spilled water. She liked the way his messy hair hung over the back of his collar.

Absentmindedly, she reached for the key he had given her. She didn't think she would ever stop loving him. He was everything she'd always hoped for, and again she wanted to pinch herself to make sure everything was real. No one was going to take him from her.

She cleared her throat. "Coffee sure smells good."

"Good morning, Luv." His head snapped around. "I trust you slept well." He smiled but didn't give her a chance to answer. "I see you found something to wear." He winked. "Most becoming."

"I hope you don't mind."

"Mind? Of course not." He straightened up. "I rather like the idea of you in my clothes . . . and bed." He chuckled as his eyes roamed possessively over her figure.

"Devon." She felt her face grow warm, and not

knowing what else to say she merely asked. "Can I help you?"

"Why don't you put out the eating utensils."

Kathy found the silverware easily. She had wondered what she would say this morning. How she would act. This definitely wasn't a normal situation for her, but Devon had already put her completely at ease. To look at him, you'd have thought she appeared half-naked in his kitchen every morning. Then again, maybe he didn't find her as appealing this morning as he did last night when he'd been drinking. She bit her bottom lip as she agonized with her ever-surfacing doubts.

As they sat down to eat, he commented, "Did you know we were on the outskirts of Hurricane Sue?"

"Really." She reached for a muffin. "No wonder it was raining cats and dogs. That also explains your inability to hang onto the umbrella." She smiled at his frown. "Did the storm do any major damage?"

"The radio announcer said all the damage was minor. It seems the storm skirted the coast and went back out into the gulf." Devon refilled their coffee mugs and they continued chatting and making small talk.

Kathy watched him over her cup. It was amazing how easily they could talk about any subject. He had not only developed into the love of her life, but also her bestfriend without her realizing it.

She took her last sip of coffee. "Breakfast was good. Is there nothing you don't do well?"

Devon turned toward her and gave her a wicked grin. "I believe there was one thing we were in question of the other night. How did I rate compared to the spaghetti?"

Kathy laughed at his easy humor. "Well--" She looked up to the ceiling as if she was giving the matter plenty of thought before she answered. "I never thought I'd love anything more than spaghetti . . . until last night." She reached over and placed her hand on his. "I believe you won . . . hands down."

"Ah, my self-esteem has been reestablished." His expression grew serious. "All kidding aside, I had a wonderful evening." He cupped her chin and brushed her lips with his.

"I did, too." She watched his eyes darken with desire. Maybe she didn't look so bad this morning. "Thank you for all my presents and especially my lovely necklace." She reached down and held the key up.

"Do you like it?"

"How could I not love such a gift? It's beautiful and because you gave it to me, it will always be treasured." A lump formed in her throat. "But will this key unlock your heart?"

"Only in the right hands." His gaze locked with hers, and his voice grew tender. "I do love you, Kathy."

"Please, Devon!" Kathy pulled away and stood up. "Don't say such things if you don't mean it. What if I gain my weight back?" She looked him straight in the eyes. "You'll be looking elsewhere, and I wouldn't blame you one bit. I can't stand the thoughts of having you for a little while then losing you. It would hurt too much." She turned away from him.

Devon's hand caught her arm and spun her around. "Stop it. I don't ever want to hear you running yourself down again. Evidently, someone has drilled into your head that you're an unworthy person. True, I don't want you to gain your weight back, but if you do my feelings will not change. I loved the person you were even before you lost the weight!" He pointed to her chest. "Do you hear me, Kathy? Do you understand?"

"Yes, I hear you. But I'm almost afraid to love you," she admitted softly. "It's too soon. Everything just seems too good to be true."

Devon reached down and lifted the key that nestled between her breasts. "Do you see this?" She nodded. "It belonged to my grandmother. It's a treasured heirloom, and I wouldn't have given it to just anybody."

Kathy looked at him with brimming eyes. She never dreamed he'd given her something so valuable. Just maybe her life was taking a turn for the better instead of the worse like it usually did. Some sixth sense told her he meant what he had said. "I love you, too," her words rushed out.

He enfolded her in his arms and she could feel all her defenses crumbling as his lips lowered to hers. His hands moved possessively over her bottom and as usual she melted against him. This could only be heaven.

The doorbell rang. Kathy jerked, startled by the bell, then she pulled back. "Have you ever noticed I hear bells every time I kiss you."

His dark eyes shined with passion before it was replaced with irritation. "I'm not expecting anyone," he grumbled as he moved through the washroom to the door.

"Hi Darling, I stopped by on my way from the airport to let you know I'm back. I can't believe you've moved into this dinky apartment." The female voice grew louder as she swept past Devon into the kitchen.

"Did you have a nice trip, Whitney?" Devon asked from behind her.

"Yes." She turned back to him before fully entering the

kitchen. "By the way, I bumped into your client's wife. You know, the one we had dinner with."

"That's good, but why are you here?"

Whitney continued on to the kitchen. "I knew you didn't mean what you said bef--" she broke off as she finally took her gaze off Devon and realized Kathy was in the room.

"Oops," Whitney gasped. "I didn't know you were entertaining a client." Her tone instantly became chilly.

"I believe you know Kathy."

"I think we've met." It took Whitney a few minutes to regain her composure as her icy eyes swept over Kathy. Evidently, Whitney had noticed what few clothes Kathy had on and she didn't bother to hide the disgust in her eyes. "Since you have a business deal here, I'll run along." She abruptly turned and hurried back to the door. "You know where I can be reached."

"Bye." She heard Devon say before be lowered his voice and said something else to Whitney.

Kathy didn't know if she felt victorious or humiliated. Whitney seemed to have the knack for making her feel dirty. Then she remembered how Whitney treated her the first day at the Country Club . . . like Kathy wasn't worthy of Devon's attention. Now she could have the last laugh because Devon loved her and had just said so. Yet, Whitney acted like she was still dating Devon. Did this mean Kathy would lose him now that his old girlfriend was back?

She watched as he walked back toward her. He didn't act upset, nor did he look guilty. Kathy shook her doubts away. It must be her overactive imagination losing control again.

"Sorry about the intrusion."

"What did Whitney mean about you living here?" Kathy grabbed the plates off the bar and placed them in the sink. "Where should you be living?"

"I have a house that I'm in the process of remodeling. It has been a bigger undertaking than I first imagined. I finally had to move to get out of the worker's way. Someday, I'll take you over and you can see my white elephant."

"I'd like that, but for now I guess it's time I should be going home."

"So soon, my Luv. I could think of a few other things we could do," he suggested as he swung her up in his arms.

Kathy decided she liked his suggestion much better than hers.

DEVON DIDN'T LEAVE when he returned Kathy to her new home. Instead he spent the day with her helping her buy groceries under his stern guidance. She decided he was her strength. Her guiding light. He made Kathy read each label to see how much fat was in the items she purchased. Devon picked out two T-bones and had them cut one and half inches thick. He said they would be good on the grill tonight. Then they bought fruit and vegetables, but he wouldn't let her go down the candy aisle at all. And when he found a pack of malted milk balls at the checkout, he frowned and handed them to the clerk. Kathy merely shrugged and claimed she had no earthly idea how they got into her cart.

Then it was off to the paint store where they purchased paint, brushes, rollers and satin-white paint. Kathy had mentioned she wanted to paint the house and Devon said he'd be glad to get her off to a good start.

When they returned home, she put on a pair of old jeans and pulled her hair back into pigtails. Rolling up her sleeves while she walked back to the living room, she smiled at the sight of Devon, bent over the gallon paint can, stirring the liquid at a slow pace.

"I appreciate you volunteering to help me." Kathy resisted the urge to slap his well-shaped rear, but instead picked up a paintbrush.

Devon laid the stirring stick to the side then poured the fresh paint in a pan. "With both of us working, we'll knock this out in no time." He straightened. "Besides, I need to work off that big steak I intend to eat tonight. I can taste those onions and mushrooms now."

"In that case . . ." Kathy laughed as she handed him a roller. "You take one wall, and I'll take the other."

By the end of the day, they had finished the living room and hallway. Devon stood back and admired their handiwork. Everything did look much better and, surprisingly, he'd enjoyed doing something so simple. He wanted to laugh as he thought of the army of painters he had employed to paint his house. And here he stood paint-splattered and loving every minute of it. Wasn't love grand?

Devon turned just as Kathy laid down her paintbrush. He could tell by the way she rubbed her arm she was tired. As she moved toward him, he grinned. She had paint streaked through her brown hair, smudged on her cheek, and splattered on her clothes.

"I'm glad you got some of the paint on the wall," he teased.

"It's amazing how much fun this was when we started . . . It's also amazing how fast the fun part wore off." Kathy massaged the back of her neck.

"Why don't you go and start dinner?" Devon suggested and I'll clean up.

"That sounds good to me."

THEY HAD JUICY T-BONE STEAKS, hot baked potatoes and rabbit food on the side -- otherwise known as salad. For desert Kathy served fresh strawberries and cream. However, her heart was with the bag of malted milk balls she'd left at the store. Since the living room smelled like paint, they sat in the kitchen drinking their coffee. Now was a good time for Kathy to find out a little more about Devon. After all, she really didn't know anything about his relationship with her great aunt.

"How did you meet my aunt?"

"We were taking the same law class." He looked at her quizzically. "I bet you didn't know your aunt frequently took college courses. I believe she said it helped to keep her mind sharp as a tack."

"No, I must confess, I didn't. She was almost eighty but appeared much younger and could always do anything." Kathy sat her coffee cup down. "You have to understand, when I was little I was constantly being shoved toward Aunt Catherine because I was her namesake. Everyone was so bad about teasing me, I began to resent her. She was older than dirt even back then. I'd love to know how many times she pinched my cheek."

Devon laughed at her remark. "You paint a completely different picture from the woman I knew."

Kathy freshened up their coffee. "Well, I would imagine that if I could have put my childhood aside and met her when I was older I might have liked her, too."

"You would have, Luv. She was simply a marvelous lady. When I was a green, young attorney and really struggling, I'd come over and have dinner with her. As a matter of fact, we'd sit at this same table. Some nights I would do a dress rehearsal for my closing arguments. You know, you remind me a lot of your aunt in many ways. You have her eyes and strong chin."

"Really. Maybe that's why I was named for her."

"I guess you're right. But I must say, she always cheered me up or gave me a dressing down when I didn't come up to her high expectations. She instilled confidence in me to get back into the fight. With her on my side, I never lost a court argument."

"I can't imagine you ever being hesitant."

"I don't know. I lived in a foreign country determined not to depend on my family. I washed plenty of dishes before I got out of school. Something my family would have definitely frowned upon."

Kathy thought that was a strange statement. Surely, he helped his mother do dishes back home, but she didn't bother to elaborate. "You always seem so sure of yourself."

Devon leaned across the table and took her hand. "I didn't think you'd believe me when I first met you, but I had a weight problem once."

"You're right. I don't believe you."

"See."

"But look at you."

"When I was in my teens, I was quite a chubby lad. At seventeen, I finally started playing sports and eating healthier foods, and it wasn't long before I shed the extra pounds. So I know how difficult controlling those urges of yours can be."

Kathy got up and walked around the table to stand in front of him. "I wouldn't have believed you."

"But you do now?" He got to his feet and pulled her to him.

"Yes, but I must say it's hard to picture you as a butterball." She looked at him impishly. "You wouldn't happen to have a picture of you, would you? You know . . . just for proof." Smiling, she patted his stomach then put her arms around his waist before looking up into his eyes. She could feel his irresistible sexual magnetism. "You know those uncontrollable urges you spoke of?"

He stared down at her upturned face and searched her eyes. He nodded at the hungry passion in her eyes before giving her a devilish grin.

"I think I have one of those urges coming on, but it's not for food." She smiled and buried her face against his throat.

Devon chuckled. Then lowered his head and whispered, his breath hot against her ear. "I think I might have just the thing to satisfy your urge."

His warm lips touched hers and a tingling spread over her as her arms went around his neck. Devon's mouth sought the warmth of hers and his arms tightened when he found it brought her closer to his body.

Her skin tingled from his sexy words. "But is it fattening?"

He scooped her up in his arms and started for the bedroom. "I promise you will not gain an ounce, my wicked girl."

CHAPTER 11

The next four weeks were the best Kathy had ever spent. She and Devon enjoyed every minute. They exercised together, ate together, but still kept separate apartments. Kathy had started painting and soon landed a contract with the Wildlife Department. Her assignment was to capture the bayous and birds of Louisiana in oil and watercolors. Life was truly wonderful.

It was October twenty-ninth and Kathy had just taken a break from her watercolors to get a cup of hot chocolate when the phone rang.

"Hi Kat!" There was a moment of silence. "It's Jack. Don't tell me you forgot your old partner so soon."

It took Kathy's mind a few minutes to register. "It's been so long, Jack. How have you been? And has Old Man Wood been his cantankerous self?"

"After you left he got worse." Jack chuckled, then added, "If that's possible. I probably should have smacked your boyfriend in the mouth because I ended up doing your work and mine, too."

Kathy felt guilty because she'd left three unfinished projects. "I'm sorry."

"And you should be. While you were throwing up your feet at the spa, I was busting my rear."

Kathy started laughing. "You poor boy. If it will make you feel any better, I didn't get to throw my feet up while I was at Weatherford. I was too busy hiking five miles every day!"

"Well, that does make me feel a little better." Jack admitted. "So tell me how are you doing?"

"I'm great. Wonderful!" she boasted. "And you should see me. I'm down to a size nine."

"Way to go. How are things with Mr. Wonderful? I must say you sound happy."

"I am, Jack." Kathy sighed. "I love Devon, and he loves me. Can you believe it?"

"That's great, Kat. If you're happy, then I'm happy for you."

"You've been a good friend for a long time. But why did you wait so long to call?"

"Well you're not the only one to find Mr. Wonderful. I found Miss Wonderful and kind of got sidetracked. But when Old Man Wood walked in with one of your paintings, I knew I had to check up on you."

"What was he doing with one of my pictures?"

"He was actually bragging on how good you are. He said he wanted to remember giving you your start."

"Sounds like him. I'm so glad you called," she said sincerely. "Please stay in touch."

"You got it. Talk to you later, Kat."

After hearing from Jack, Kathy felt energized. She spent the rest of the morning in her studio, but promised herself she'd stop by and have lunch with him one day soon. Jack had been her first friend when she moved to New Orleans.

These last few months she'd kept herself isolated though she hadn't realized that fact until now. But she'd been so happy she really hadn't thought about anyone else except Tina, and Kathy wasn't ready to see her sister just yet. Her mother called the other day to lecture her about the way she had treated her sister. Kathy wanted to respond with *how about the way she treats me*, but instead she just listened. It was strange, her mother hadn't even asked how *she* was doing with her weight loss. The whole conversation had been about Tina.

Kathy had always wondered why Tina was her mother's favorite. Sometimes Kathy thought of herself as a stray left on their doorstep. Thinking back, her dad and Aunt Catherine were the only ones to show they had cared about her. Her mother ended the conversation by saying she and Dad were going to Europe for a couple of months.

Checking her watch, Kathy started to clean her paintbrushes. Devon was playing in a tennis match at the Country Club. It was a benefit for the Cancer Foundation and started at four o'clock. She had just enough time to change clothes.

ARRIVING AT THE CLUB, she spotted Devon's car and parked beside it. Kathy was surprised at the hundreds who had turned out for the charity event. Then she remembered the wealthy didn't have to punch a time clock.

Kathy was standing next to the shrubs, trying to decide where to sit when she heard someone mention Devon's name. Glancing to her left, she saw the top of two female heads who evidently were having a conversation about Devon. Since they couldn't see her from where she stood, she remained to listen. It didn't take long before Kathy recognized Whitney's voice.

"He's living in the smallest apartment you've ever seen."

"But why?"

"I couldn't believe it," Whitney commented to her friend. "He has that beautiful estate, and yet he has moved into a tiny apartment. When I asked him, he said he was having the whole thing remodeled. But I'm not so sure that's true."

"What do you mean?"

"I think Devon is hard up for money."

"How can that be? He's a successful lawyer."

Precisely what Kathy was thinking.

"He might have a good law practice, but he has an expensive car, two houses, and he gambles. After a while everything begins to add up. The last few times he's been to see me, we stayed at the house and didn't go anywhere," Whitney complained.

Kathy's eyes grew wide. Whitney was lying. Devon hadn't been to see her.

"But I thought he was dating that other woman." The other woman spoke with disbelief in her voice.

"He is. But wouldn't you if you could smell a lot of money coming your way," Whitney said smugly.

There was a gasp. "What do you mean?"

"Devon will pick up any stray. Besides that old woman is making it well worth his efforts. She's paying him to be nice to that girl. Why else would he be doing it."

"Really?"

Kathy felt as if all the blood had been drained from

her body. She had heard enough. Numbness covered her body and she had to concentrate hard so she wouldn't collapse as she made her way to the bleachers. Somehow the day didn't look so bright and pretty anymore. She clenched her hands to keep them from trembling. Finally, she found a seat in the sixth row and sat down to watch the tennis match.

Devon reared back and served a perfect ace. He bounced the ball several times then looked up and scanned the crowd before his next serve. Kathy waved and saw his return smile. He had looked for her. Didn't that mean something? She watched as he volleyed skillfully back and forth.

Maybe that was what she loved most about Devon -- his confidence. Kathy wished she'd had more of that a few minutes ago. What she should have done was walk around the bush and confronted Whitney and accused her of lying. Whitney just had to be lying!

Devon had spent every night with her except for a couple of times when he had worked late. But wouldn't she know if he were cheating? Kathy had detected no change in him. She knew there were men who ran scams on women all the time. But her Devon couldn't be one of them. She had to have more proof than mere gossip. Maybe there was some way she could see her aunt's will and verify if there were provisions that would benefit Devon. Just thinking that he could be deceitful made her feel terribly guilty for doubting him.

Her attention was drawn back to the game when Devon walked over to the net and shook hands with his opponent. He had won, of course. A sudden chill ran over Kathy as she stood to clap. Devon always won.

Devon turned and motioned for her to come down.

When she reached him he said, "I was beginning to think you were not coming."

"I only missed the first couple of serves." She stared at his shirt not able to look into his eyes. "I never dreamed there would be so many people here. I had trouble finding a seat."

"That would explain why I lost my first two serves." He smiled and placed his knuckle under her chin. "I needed you for luck."

"Thank you." She raised her eyes, hoping she didn't look guilty from her previous thought. She managed a smile. "Are we going to stay for the other matches?"

"If you don't mind, Luv, I'm kind of tired." He slipped his arm around her waist. "Why don't we go home?"

Now was her chance. "Speaking of home . . . I heard someone mention your estate. I think it's time you showed me your other home."

Devon looked down at her quizzically before saying, "I wanted to wait until all the renovations were complete before I let you see Bridgewell, but I guess it won't hurt to give you a sneak preview."

"This must be some place if it has a name."

"Just a modest estate, Luv, and you'll soon see why it carries such a name. Come on, I'll drive."

They rode for about fifteen minutes into the country before Devon made a left turn onto a gravel road. There were absolutely no other houses in sight as they drove a half mile down the lane. "You're terribly quiet today," Devon commented.

Kathy's doubts stabbed through her like a knife. She felt guilty doubting him. Relationships were built on love and trust, she kept saying to herself. "I have a slight headache," she lied to cover the truth. Then her eyes opened wide. "Look!" She pointed up ahead. "I can't remember the last time I've seen a covered bridge."

"Precisely," Devon said as they drove through the gray covered bridge. "Now look to your right."

On top of the hill, sat an old-timey well complete with bucket and crank. "I see," she laughed. "-- bridge -- well. I bet you picked out the name."

"If only I could take credit; however, the previous owners chose the lovely title."

They drove another half mile before the house came into view. Pulling into a circular driveway that had a water fountain in the middle, Devon drove the car to the front of the biggest house she'd ever seen. "This is yours?"

"Mine and the bank's, Luv." He switched off the motor and opened his door. "Come, I'll show you around."

They entered high, double, black walnut doors into a round circular entryway that encased a winding staircase leading to the upper floors. Oversized windows and seventeen-foot ceilings provided a breathtaking view. Each room they entered was more impressive than the last even if it was viewed through the many scaffolds that were everywhere. An expansive master suite spanned the first floor complete with a whirlpool and small office. "This must be costing a fortune," Kathy whispered, almost afraid to speak aloud in the majestic surroundings.

Devon watched Katherine as her eyes grew wide. He could see how impressed she looked and it made him proud. It was on the tip of his tongue to ask her how she would like her new home once it was completed, but that would have to wait for later. Tomorrow night he intended to ask Katherine to be his wife.

"You might say I've spent a bit of change on this home. Do you like it?"

"Beautiful doesn't even begin to describe this place. How in the world did you ever find it?"

"A client of mine needed to sell before he returned to Scotland. And upon seeing the roominess, I just couldn't resist. There are huge floor-to-ceiling windows in every room, which help me feel a part of nature. It's so peaceful when I'm out here away from the hustle and bustle of the city."

"I can understand how you feel."

"By the way." Devon put his arm around Kathy as they moved to the front door. "We are invited to a masquerade party tomorrow at the Blake's. They are one of my clients. So you need to be thinking of a good costume."

"Well I can't go as Humpty Dumpty anymore."

Devon chuckled. "No. But you would make a ravishing Cinderella."

KATHY FINISHED PAINTING the last red circle on her cheek, then slipped on her red mop top hair. Tonight she would go as Raggedy Ann. Maybe hiding behind her disguise she'd get up enough nerve to ask to see a copy of her aunt's will. She had tried to do so on the way home from Bridgewell, but couldn't get the words out.

Devon's home had been more lavish than she had ever dreamed. It had to have set him back a good half million. He definitely had expensive taste, but again she found herself questioning could he afford everything? Did lawyers make that kind of money. Kathy held her head, wishing these doubts would go away and leave her in peace.

The doorbell rang. Kathy sighed with relief. She looked

forward to getting out of the house and away from the demons that were trying to spoil her happiness.

She answered the door and immediately started to laugh. The real Prince Charming stood on her threshold dressed in honest to goodness pantaloons. "It's wonderful!" She shook her head and dabbed the corners of her eyes, catching the moisture gathered there. "You are bound to win first prize."

"Thank you, madam." Devon bowed from the waist. "And where is my princess? I see before me a rag doll."

"It was either this or a dancing bear. I'm afraid the costume shop didn't have much to choose from by the time I got there."

His eyes glowed with amusement. "You made a wise choice then." He leaned over to kiss her, but between the white grease paint and glaring red spots, he couldn't find a clear spot. He simply shook his head and said, "Let's go."

They drove slowly, watching out for the trick-or-treaters. The children walked on the sidewalks dressed as ghost and goblins and carrying bags or pumpkins. "Look, Devon. Aren't they adorable?"

He slowed down a little more as they watched two small tots trying to climb a rather steep set of stairs. It seemed to be a hard climb as they balanced their pump-kins laden with candy. Devon glanced over at Kathy's radiant smile and sparkling eyes. Without thinking, he asked, "Would you like to have children?"

Kathy swung around. Her gold-flecked eyes grew wide with surprise. "Right this minute?" Her features became more animated, and he saw a flash of humor cross her face.

"Well," he turned up his smile a notch before he started driving again. "That could be arranged."

"Yes, but then we would miss your party," she teased.

"Be serious. Do you want children?"

"I never gave it much thought," Kathy admitted. "Because I never intended to get married."

"You don't have to get married to have children."

"I do. And in answer to your question, I like children, but I don't think I would be the type of person who would marry and say we must have 2.9 kids like everyone else." Devon chuckled, and Kathy hit him on the arm. "I'm serious. I'd marry for love and down the road if I became pregnant I'd be happy. But I must confess I can't imagine myself being a mother."

They pulled up into the Blake's driveway where a valet walked over to the driver's side. Devon turned to Kathy and, not bothering to hide the huskiness in his voice, he said, "I can."

THEY SQUEEZED their way into the crowded room. This reminded Kathy of the Mardi Gras though the costumes were not as elaborate and the crowd was a little calmer.

Clusters of men and women stood in various corners chatting, and Kathy wondered if she knew anyone here. If so, they were well disguised. She followed Devon between an assortment of animals, pirates, kings and queens. Kathy turned, she could have sworn she'd seen Lady Godivia a minute ago. Not paying any attention, she ran head on into the back of Devon as he stopped in front of a mummy. "Sorry," she murmured to his back.

Devon reached back and pulled her around to his side. "Kathy, I'd like you to meet my partner, Ed Wilder."

"It's nice to meet you." Her gaze swept over his

costume. "I didn't realize that Devon's partner had one foot in the grave." Her playful remark produced immediate laughter from Ed.

"That's good. I like a woman with a sense of humor. I bet Devon tells you he works all the time because I can't keep up my end. Am I right?"

Kathy opened her mouth to assure Ed that Devon did no such a thing, but Ed cut her off. "The fact is the boy loves money."

Her mind blurred at the reference to money. God, she felt like she was going crazy. She had to put these doubts to rest. How would Devon feel if she asked to see his bank account?

"Don't paint a bad picture of me to Kathy, when it's you that has been taking on too much work."

"I hate a man who always speaks the truth," Ed confessed, then added, "speaking of money, have you seen the Blakes?"

"No, we just got here."

"Make sure you see them before you leave. They asked about you earlier."

"I'll do that but first I'd like to dance with my Raggedy Ann."

Kathy relaxed the minute Devon's arms came around her. If only she could shut out the rest of the world. Would she ever learn to trust completely? Why did she have the eerie feeling that something was going to happen?

Devon missed the scent of her hair as he laid his cheek on Kathy's mop top. He had planned to ask Katherine to marry him tonight. It would be perfect with him dressed as Prince Charming but every time he looked at her white face and bright red cheeks all he could do was laugh. Since he had known his little rag doll, she had brought nothing but happiness to his life.

All too soon the song ended and Devon reluctantly removed his arms from around Kathy. Taking her by the elbow, he guided her toward the Blakes.

"Great party, Adam," Devon said.

"Glad you could come," Blake shook his head.

A lady, who Kathy assumed must be Mrs. Blake, grabbed her arm. "Whitney, this reminds me of our first meeting at the Charter House. I thought it was going to be another boring business dinner that stuffy July night, but you saved me. I'm glad to see this man of yours is keeping you happy."

"Ann," Devon cleared this throat. "This isn't Whitney. I'd like you to meet Kathy Taylor."

"Oh . . . my. I'm so sorry I just thought . . . the last time we met Devon he had Wh-- so I assumed," Mrs. Blake couldn't seem to stop her rattling. "You must think I'm terrible, dear."

Kathy's stomach had twisted itself into a knot. However, her voice showed little of the emotion that ran rampant over her body. "I'm not sure my own mother would recognize me in this costume."

Devon felt the stiffness in Kathy's arm. He knew she was thinking all the wrong things. This whole scene could have been avoided if he'd simply told Kathy about their dinner meeting. "I haven't dated Whitney in a long time, Ann."

"I'm sorry if I offended you, Kathy," Ann tried one more time to apologize.

"Don't worry about it." Kathy brushed her off.

Adam Blake butted into the conversation. "Devon, I'd

like to see you in the morning. I have some paperwork I need your opinion on."

"I'll tell my secretary to pencil you in at ten."

Devon tightened his grip on Kathy and steered her away from the Blakes. He needed someplace private to talk to her.

"I want to go home," Kathy told him.

"Are you sure you want to leave so soon?"

"Yes," Kathy snapped unable to keep the emotion out of her voice. "I'll call a cab if you want to stay."

"Nonsense. I brought you, and I will take you home."

The car was quickly brought around and they were on their way. This time neither noticed the trick-a-treaters. And neither said a word.

Finally, Devon broke the silence. "I think I need to explain Ann's remark."

"What's there to explain? You took Whitney out while you had me conveniently tucked away at Weatherford." Kathy felt like a pressure cooker that had just reached its boiling point. "You went to a lot of expense to get me out of your hair when all you had to do was tell me you loved her."

They pulled into the driveway as Devon snapped. "You're being unreasonable. I don't love Whitney. I've told you before that I love you."

Angry, Kathy only heard the unreasonable remark. "Unreasonable! Yes, I was unreasonable to think that I could trust you. I found out yesterday you've been seeing Whitney at the same time words of love came tumbling out of your mouth." Kathy took a gasp of air. As she did, her dream flared before her eyes. *It was for the money, Kathy, only the money.* She shook her head to free the image and with that what little reasoning she had left.

Tears streaked down her white face paint as she grabbed for the door handle. Before getting out she turned to Devon. "It was always the money, wasn't it?"

Anger flared in Devon's eyes. His jaw clenched so tightly a nerve had begun to twitch. Gone was the face that had made her so happy. She expected him to blow up in a rage or at least deny her accusations. Instead he looked at her with eyes as cold as ice. "You seem to have all the answers. There is nothing left for me to say."

Kathy felt herself grow cold inside as his words slapped her in the face, but his final words pierced her heart.

"Get out!"

CHAPTER 12

*K*athy's hands trembled as she slipped the key into the lock. Tires squealed behind her, and she turned in time to glimpse Devon's fading taillights.

As she fumbled for the light switch, it seemed like forever before her fingers made contact. Her stage makeup had begun to run and burn her eyes. She slammed the door, jarring the pictures on the walls. Blinded by tears, she yanked off her Raggedy Ann wig as she stumbled up the stairs. Why had she thought this time would be any different from the rest? Her relationships were always doomed.

Men were all alike. She'd be better off without any of them. Unbuttoning her costume, Kathy threw it aside and went to the sink where she scrubbed off the remains of her painted-on smile. She took two aspirin for her pounding headache then went into the bedroom. Before climbing into bed, she grabbed a box of tissue.

The night grew long. She was plagued with visions of Devon. One minute he'd hold her in his arms, then just when she'd begun to relax laughter would erupt and he'd tell her what a fool she had been. She woke herself with her screams. Only when she calmed down did she realize it had all been a dream and she was alone.

Always alone.

By the next morning, Kathy's eyelids were so swollen she could hardly open them. She wondered if she'd ever run out of tears.

Slowly she sat up. Throbbing pains shot through her head, but they were nothing compared to the ache in her heart. She tried to piece together what had happened last night. Mrs. Blake had confirmed that Devon had in fact dated Whitney while Kathy was gone. Did that mean that everything between them had been a lie. Devon had always seemed so sensitive . . . could she have been that wrong?

If only he had explained.

If only she had let him.

Guilt swept over Kathy as she climbed out of bed. He had tried to explain, but she'd cut him off. Now she would never know what he was going to say. Perhaps it was just as well. It would have been more lies.

Half-heartedly, she dressed and went downstairs to make coffee. What was she going to do when she felt like doing nothing? Keeping busy would keep her mind off things. Besides, her eyes were so swollen she couldn't go anywhere. Propping her chin up with her hand, Kathy thought a few minutes while she drank her tasteless coffee. What would she do today? She had wanted to clean out Aunt Catherine's room; now she couldn't think of a better time.

The morning went by slowly as Kathy packed away the last of her aunt's clothes. She had to admit the woman had great taste.

Glancing back at the empty closet, Kathy saw a square

brown box. She walked over and picked up the small suitcase. Snapping the lock, she lifted the lid. The box contained papers, and on the very top was a copy of Aunt Catherine's will. Kathy had wanted proof and now it had been dumped in her lap.

She glanced up to heaven. Was this some divine answer from above?

Moving back over to the wingback chair, Kathy set the box down beside the chair, but she remained standing. A part of her wanted to know and a part of her didn't. What if Devon was as devious as she had been lead to believe? Would she ever be able to trust anyone again?

Stooping down, she picked up the blue-covered document, then sighed. Now she would have some answers, but not before she had another cup of coffee. She needed something to steady her nerves.

Returning with a cup and saucer, Kathy placed them on the small round table next to her and picked up the will. She read through all the boring legal talk, recognizing the parts Devon had read to her. Then she turned over to the last page and surprisingly, there was nothing. Slowly, she laid the document down and picked up her cup. A fleeting small smile crossed her lips before she took a sip of hot coffee. There were no stipulations for Devon. He wouldn't gain anything by her meeting the conditions of the will. As a matter of fact, there was a stamp at the bottom of the will that said, "Fee . . . no charge." He hadn't even charged Aunt Katherine for drawing up the will.

So if money had nothing to do with it, could Whitney just be spreading malicious gossip? Had Whitney played her for a fool? Kathy had been so naive she had played right into her hands?

Kathy thought back to last night. What had she said?

She remembered Devon had tried to explain, but she cut him off. She wasn't quite sure of all the nasty things she had said, but she knew it had been pretty bad.

And she had been wrong . . . so wrong. Tears sprang to her eyes and she shut them tight. The look on Devon's face had not been pleasant when he told her to get out of his car. There had been no pain or hatred in his eyes. They had been dull, cold and unforgiving. He had to know people said things when they were angry that they really didn't mean. Maybe he would call today after he cooled off.

Wiping away her tears, Kathy went back to the small suitcase and pulled out another handful of papers. There was the title to Aunt Catherine's car, marriage certificate, bonds and CD's. Then Kathy pulled out a yellowed parchment tied in pink ribbon. She slipped off the ribbon and unfolded it. In the bottom left hand corner, there was a set of tiny footprints, and Kathy knew automatically it was a birth certificate. She searched for the date, figuring it must the Aunt Catherine's birth record. September 15, 1970 was sprawled in blue ink. "Strange, that's my birthday." Kathy looked at the child's name. Katherine Ann spelled with a K. And the mother's name was Catherine Dubois and the father's name Charles Dubois.

"This is my birth certificate. But it doesn't make any sense." She looked one more time to find Aunt Catherine's age. She was 52. My God, Aunt Catherine was her real mother!

Kathy reached for the phone to call her mother, then remembered her parents had left the country. She drew her shaking hand back slowly, feeling completely numb inside. How could they have tossed her around like a ball? Why couldn't somebody have loved her? Suddenly, the room started to spin. She wasn't real! Her life wasn't real. She wasn't even sure who she was anymore. Kathy had always thought her mother -- or who she thought was her mother --had loved Tina the most.

Kathy sighed and wiped her tears away. There would be no immediate answers, but since she was falling apart anyway it didn't matter. She just didn't care anymore.

Nothing mattered.

Kathy sat staring at the distant wall. She wasn't sure how much time had passed before she looked again at the papers in her lap. She lacked definite answers, but she assumed she was a mid-life baby and Aunt Catherine gave her away because of her age. Kathy started to put the papers on the floor when a picture fell out. She turned the photo over and recognized a young girl who could have been her twin. Now everything seemed to fall in place.

No wonder she had always felt like an outsider with her mother. And it also explained the extra attention from Aunt Catherine. Kathy thought of the way she'd treated her aunt and a new round of tears burned her already red, swollen eyes.

If she could turn back the clock, she would have treated her differently. She had to stop this crying or her eyes would be swollen completely shut, and she'd need a seeing eye dog to lead her about. But with her luck, the dog would run off and leave her like everybody else had. Damn, she had a bad case of feeling sorry for herself, but then why shouldn't she . . . nobody else would. Wiping her eyes and blowing her nose, Kathy continued her search. There was one more document left in the bottom of the small suitcase. As she reached for it, she glanced at the clock. It was mid-afternoon, but time really didn't matter anymore. What did she have to do?

God, she was pathetic!

The last piece of paper was a letter from the Marquess of Edgewood addressed to Aunt Catherine. She actually had known royalty. Was there nothing this woman hadn't done? Kathy was beginning to see her in a different light -- someone interesting -- someone who had traveled -- someone who had loved her very much.

> *Dear Catherine,*
> *We want to thank you for keeping an eye out for our*
> *son. He's such a head-strong lad who's*
> *determined to deny his lineage.*
>
> *Thanks for being a friend.*
> *Devon York*
> *Marquess of Edgewood*

SO IT HADN'T BEEN a coincidence that Aunt Catherine befriended Devon. He had tried so hard to do things on his own, yet his parents were keeping an eye on him all the time. And Devon was a blue blood when all the time she'd pictured his parents as being poor. Kathy shook her head. Where Devon was concerned she'd jumped to all the wrong conclusions.

He'd offered her friendship. She wanted more.

When he offered her more, she asked why.

THREE DAYS PASSED and still no phone call from Devon. By Friday Kathy couldn't stand it any longer, she picked up the phone and dialed his office. She'd just beg for his forgiveness and swear never to doubt him again.

"Good morning. Dudley, Smith and York, may I help you?"

"Linda, may I speak to Devon." Kathy had long since quit identifying herself to the receptionist.

"I'm sorry, he's tied up at the moment."

"Will you ask him to call me."

"Sure will."

Kathy knew his meetings usually were long, so she went out and bought a few groceries. As soon as she returned she checked the answering machine. A steady red light confirmed there were no messages. She busied herself cleaning up the house, but constantly her eyes strayed to the clock. She even picked up the phone a couple of times to make sure it was working. By four o'clock, she couldn't stand the wait any longer. She snatched up the receiver and punched in the numbers.

"Good afternoon. Dudley, Smith and York, may I help you?"

"Did you give Devon my message?" Kathy blurted out.

"Yes, I did."

"Well, he didn't call back. Is he in now?"

"I'm sorry, Kathy. But Mr. York instructed me to take messages if you called. I--I tried to get him to call, but he said he didn't wish to speak with you."

Kathy choked with hurt that stabbed through her. He didn't want to talk to her. "I see," she barely managed to get out before dropping the phone.

Boy, had she screwed up this time. The one thing that had happened good in her life and she'd managed destroy the relationship. She had taken the love Devon had offered and thrown it in his face. Why hadn't she believed him?

Yet, he was now doing the same thing she had done, judging her without hearing the whole truth.

She looked over at the kitchen counter and spotted the bag of malted milk balls she hadn't resisted buying. Tearing open the bag, she began to pop them in her mouth one by one, but by the time she had eaten a dozen, Kathy realized they were not giving her the pleasure she needed. Devon had even taken away the one thing she used to enjoy.

Picking up the bag, she slung it across the room, sending chocolate candies scattering in every direction.

"Damn you, Devon York for ever entering my life!"

FUELED BY HER ANGER, Kathy made it through the first part of November. She would paint until the wee hours of morning and then fall into an exhausted sleep. Her life seemed to be dangling by a string. Still there was no phone call from Devon.

Kathy had worked harder than usual at the spa today, trying to shed the five pounds she'd gained back. She really missed working out at the Country Club, but since she and Devon had broken up, she figured they would turn her away at the door. Besides she couldn't stand seeing Devon at a distance without talking to him.

The spa she'd joined was nice enough, and determined to reach her goal, Kathy had doubled her exercise sets. A couple of men had asked her out which had bolstered her ego, but she had turned them down. The only thing the spa didn't have was Devon . . . the one thing she still wanted more than anything.

"I'm thirsty," Kathy said to herself as she pulled into a

parking space at the Greek Garden. She'd just get a drink before she went home. They had good fountain sodas, and Kathy always treated herself if she'd had a good workout.

Pulling into the parking space, she turned off the motor and raised the sun visor. Slowly her hand fell to her lap. In the big picture window sat a group of four men. But only one person held her attention. Dressed in white, his dark hair appeared wind-blown as if he'd spent the day playing tennis, which he probably had. Devon looked wonderful.

God, how she missed him. She missed the way he laughed and the tender way he'd held her. As she stared at him, he turned and their eyes locked. Kathy wanted to look away, embarrassed that she'd been caught staring at him like a love-sick puppy. It had been a month since she'd seen him. A month, she wanted to laugh, it seemed more like a lifetime.

Devon didn't smile. He merely stared. But she caught just a touch of pain in his eyes before it was replaced with a blank stare. He had changed, Kathy noticed. His face was thinner and there was no laughter in his eyes. They were dull, hollow and cold. He had been working too hard. She'd bet her life on that fact. But did he miss her? Had she made some difference in his life?

Kathy felt as if she would melt under his scrutiny. "I'm so sorry, Devon," she murmured. "If only I could take back all the hateful things I said."

Suddenly, the other three men turned around to see what held Devon's attention. Kathy felt herself flush under the four pair of eyes. She glanced down and grabbed her purse.

Opening the car door, she couldn't resist sneaking a peek at the window again. Devon had returned his attention not back to his buddies, but to Whitney who stood beside him with her arms casually draped across his shoulder.

Whitney . . . It was always Whitney. Jealousy twisted Kathy's insides. She moved to the front door of the restaurant with a determination born out of anger. Why should she feel guilty about anything? Evidently, Devon had no regrets. With herself out of her life, it appeared he conveniently picked up his old habits.

"Can I get you a table, ma'am?"

"No." Kathy lost her train of thought at the waiter's question. "I-I'm sorry." She shook her head. "I just want a large Coke to go, please."

She stood in the entrance tapping her foot, feeling as if she should hide just in case Devon came this way. Then as if a bolt of lightning hit her between the eyes, she said, "Hide." Why in the hell should she hide? He was the two-timing bastard, and damn if she wasn't going to tell him so . . . right now!

"Your drink, ma'am."

"I'll get it in a minute," Kathy snapped.

DEVON LISTENED to the corny joke Frank was recounting to them when he felt someone staring at him. Slowly he turned and looked out the window. His throat tightened. It was Kathy.

He could see her golden eyes as clearly as if she sat across the table for him. He was drawn to her. Lord help him, she was still in his blood.

It took all his effort not to get up and go to her. He wanted to. God, knows he wanted to know how she was doing. He longed to hear her laugh. He couldn't remember laughing much himself lately. Bloody hell. He missed her more than he ever thought possible.

His Kathy. He'd wanted so much to make her a part of his life. But she'd put an end to that because she couldn't trust him. She could never trust him. The doubts would always be between them, so it was better to keep his distance.

Would she make her goal in December? Did she really have the guts to carry it through without his help? He almost smiled. Had he been helping her, or had she been helping him? He honestly felt as if a part of his life was missing. A part he couldn't get back. And it had been a good part. Maybe the best.

"What in the hell has your attention?" When Frank, one of Devon's tennis buddies, didn't get an answer they all turned to see for themselves.

"Damn, if she wouldn't hold my attention, too!" Frank laughed. Devon's jaw tightened at Frank's off-hand compliment.

"Who is she?" Calvin asked.

"Someone I once thought I knew."

All three said at once, "So that's her?" They all turned to look at Devon. They all knew the story.

"Yes, that's Kathy."

"Then why aren't you with her?" Frank persisted. "It's as plain as the nose on your face that you care for that lady more than even you care to admit."

Devon didn't answer because a hand touched his arm. "Hi, Darling." Whitney smiled at the other men. "Amazing meeting you here when I was just thinking about phoning you."

"Really." Devon picked up his tea glass and took a sip.

"I'm cooking your favorite tonight. I thought you might like to come to dinner."

Devon stood. "Maybe another night, Whitney, I have plans."

As the group walked out of the restaurant, Frank punched Calvin in the side. "Can you imagine -- two beautiful women and Devon had rather play poker with us."

Calvin chuckled. "That boy's in deep trouble."

KATHY STORMED into the dining room. Determined to air her grievance to everyone in the restaurant, but when she reached Devon's table it was empty. He was gone. More than that, he was gone with *her*!

Moisture started to build in the corners of her eyes, when a waitress tapped her on the shoulder."

"Can I help you?"

"The group that was sitting here." Kathy pointed to the table. "When did they leave?"

"They left through the side door just a few minutes ago."

Kathy's anger dissipated as she went back to get her soda. The tears spilled over and trickled down her cheeks as she paid for the drink.

As the cashier handed her the change, she placed a hand on Kathy's arm and whispered, "I'm sorry, honey."

Kathy nodded and ran from the restaurant before she could embarrass herself further by sobbing.

CHAPTER 13

$\mathcal{B}$y the time Kathy reached her house, she'd became a combination of a heartbroken woman one minute and a raving lunatic the next. She needed help.

What she needed was someone to talk to. Going over to the phone, she called Jack. The minute she heard his voice she started to cry.

"Is that you, Kat?"

"Uh-huh," she managed to get out.

"Slow down and tell me what's happened."

Kathy twisted the phone cord around her finger, catching her breath. "I screwed everything up, Jack."

"Now wait a minute. It takes two to tango," he said in his calm, never-to-get-excited voice. "I'm sure it's not all your fault."

"B--but he won't t--talk to me." She hiccupped.

"Kat, I'd come to see you, but I was just walking out the door to catch a plane. I want you to regroup and get in there and fight if you still want him."

"D--do you t--think there's a chance?"

"I sure do! I'm sorry I have to leave you, Kat." He paused. "I know . . . why don't you call the girl you met at that spa."

"Mary Leigh?"

"That's the one. I bet she'll make you feel much better."

Kathy straightened in her chair. "I'll do that. You have a good trip."

Kathy did feel better after talking to Jack. She waited a few minutes for her hiccups to stop, then she didn't waste one minute picking up the phone and calling Mary Leigh.

When she answered, Kathy blurted out, "Help!"

"Kathy is that you?"

Kathy wanted to laugh. Everyone could tell who was calling just by one word. Did that mean she was always in a constant state of hysteria? "Good guess. How would you like to see your prized pupil?"

"I'd love it! I thought I was going to have to spend Thanksgiving by myself. Come spend the holidays with me at Weatherford. I could use the company." Mary Leigh sounded elated.

"I'll be there. Have they closed the five-mile torture track?" Kathy could still picture herself trudging down the endless path.

"I'm afraid not. As a matter of fact we now have two."

"Great." This time Kathy wouldn't complain about exercise. She intended to keep busy enough to forget her problems.

Forget her life. And if she was real lucky find herself.

"See you at Thanksgiving, and don't forget to bring your swimsuit."

"Is it that warm?"

"We're having a very mild winter so we can soak up some sun."

THE NEXT MORNING Kathy felt more positive than she had in a long time. She would have to have money if she was going to Weatherford. Since she'd not received a check from her painting, she would have to call Devon. She wondered if this would make him speak to her.

"Good morning, Dudley, Smith and, York. How can I help you?"

"Hi Linda. I need to get some money from my estate."

"Just a minute while I ring Mr. York."

In no time, Linda was back on the phone. "He said how much do you want?"

Kathy was galled he wouldn't get on the phone himself. How could she penetrate his cold indifference? Perhaps, she'd just give him something to think about. "I want three thousand dollars."

"Just a moment." Linda put Kathy back on hold. "He wants to know why?"

"Because it's my money and I'm going to take a trip." Kathy's voice raised an octave. "And if Mr. York wants to know where tell him it's none of his business unless he wants to get on the phone and ask me himself."

"Are you sure you want me to say that?"

"You're damn right I do. And in those exact same words!"

Again there was music. "He said he'd have a check to you in two hours."

"Thank you," Kathy told Linda. It wasn't her fault Devon was being unreasonable. But when Kathy hung, up her niceness evaporated.

"That ass! He has some nerve treating me like this." She kicked the stuffed chair and immediately jerked her foot up in pain. She had a good mind to go down to his office and collect the money in person. Then the only way he could avoid her was jumping from the window . . . if she didn't push him first.

"What is wrong with the man? He's so frustrating!" She hobbled upstairs to fix her hair. "Devon needs something to shake him out of this coma he's in."

As she picked up the brush, the light caught her necklace. The key. It had become so much a part of her that she hadn't given the gift a second thought. It was her gift of love, or so she thought.

She reached behind her neck and unfastened the clasp. She didn't want to get rid of it, but it meant little to her without Devon. She would send the key back with a note to his majesty. He couldn't continue avoiding her. Sometime soon he would have to speak to her . . . one way or the other.

Going to her desk, she sat down and drew out a sheet of cream-colored paper. Where should she start? For a few minutes, she could do nothing but stare at the blank sheet. She longed to pour out her heart -- to make him understand, but she would not beg for his forgiveness; she'd be blunt and to the point.

> *Devon,*
> *Because this is a valuable key and I seem to mean*
>   *nothing to you, I'm returning your gift. I'm*
>   *sorry I misjudged you. I shouldn't have listened*
>   *to malicious gossip. But now you sit in*
>   *judgement of me, so you're no better than I.*
> *I guess I wasn't the person you thought I was. And*

evidently I wasn't the one who could unlock
your heart.
Yours,
Kathy

SHE PLACED the necklace in a sheet of paper and folded the letter around it. Slipping it into an envelope, it seemed strange to Kathy that Devon hadn't already asked for the key. Of course, that meant he'd have to speak to her. With a shake of her head, Kathy sighed. She'd just save him the trouble. She sealed the envelope and prayed this would wake him up. Even if it was only to tell her to go to hell at least he'd be communicating with her.

KATHY HAD MAILED the letter on the way to the airport. She'd had barely enough time to make her gate, but she had and now was on her way to Weatherford. Her ears popped as the plane climbed to a new altitude. What would Devon think when he received her note? He could be hurt. Or would he be angry enough to hop in the car, rush over to her house, and demand she put the key back around her neck. She gazed out the plane window, resting her head on the glass. No matter what he did, she wouldn't be around to find out. She was going to rest, relax, and maybe find some kind of peace. Her emotional roller coaster had just come to an end.

Kathy couldn't wait for the plane door to open once they reached Yuma, Arizona. She walked down the long corridor, pulling her carry bag behind her. Mary Leigh was the first person Kathy spotted when she entered the terminal. Her short haircut and bright smile hadn't changed one bit, Kathy thought as she moved in her direction.

"Look at you!" Mary Leigh's eyebrows raised in amazement. "It's apparent you don't need me anymore."

"That's not true." Kathy laughed and hugged her. "I have ten more pounds to lose before Christmas, my life is a shambles, and all I do is cry. I think I need you more than ever." Kathy looped her arm through her friend's.

"Sounds serious."

"It is but I don't want to talk about it." Kathy shook her head. "For now, I just want to exercise and soak up the sun." Kathy laughed. "I bet you'd never thought I would look forward to exercising. I guess miracles happen every day."

And that's exactly what they did. For the next three days they took long walks, exercised and swam. Since the staff was off for the holidays, they had the whole place to themselves. They had a ball in the big kitchen, cooking a turkey breast for their Thanksgiving meal.

THE BREEZE CARRIED the relaxing warmth of the desert. Kathy looked over at Mary Leigh who had her face covered with a hat. They were lying out by the pool when Kathy asked, "Why aren't you spending Thanksgiving with your family?"

"They're dead, I'm afraid."

"I'm sorry to heard that." Kathy grew quiet, realizing for the first time that her real mother was dead, too. "But someone as pretty as yourself must have a boyfriend?"

"I do." Mary Leigh took off her hat and looked at

Kathy. "He's overseas and couldn't get leave to come home."

"That's too bad, but I'm pleased for myself," Kathy admitted sheepishly. "Not that I'm selfish you understand." Then she smiled.

"What about your family?" Mary Leigh asked as she picked up her glass of ice water.

"To tell you the truth, I don't know who my family is anymore."

Mary Leigh choked on the water, and Kathy patted her back. "I think you'd better explain."

And Kathy did. For the next hour, she filled her friend in on what she had found during her search through Aunt Catherine's papers. She didn't leave out anything that had happened with Devon. "Well what do you think?"

"I found the part about your family hard to believe. The woman you've been calling Mother all these years was really your aunt. You must feel like you've been watching a soap opera."

"You could say that."

"As for Devon, I'm sorry you had that silly fight, but I think you'll get his attention with the key. It sounds like the necklace could be considered an engagement ring. I think he loves you a great deal from what you've told me."

"I'm not so sure about the engagement part. Devon never mentioned anything about marriage. Yet, he was always sweet and attentive. But how do I know he wasn't like that with everyone he dated?"

"I met Devon only once when he was out here for some rest. Of course, he turned every woman's head, but he struck me as being very sincere. I'd hang on to him if I were you."

"But I'm not sure he still loves me at least he doesn't act

that way anymore. Come to think of it, I don't know how he's really acting because he won't see me." Kathy's temper rose just a notch thinking about his stubbornness.

"You don't turn love off like a spigot." Mary Leigh turned on her side and rested her head on her hand. "He's probably had his pride hurt. Think about it, Kathy. Devon probably never opened up to another woman like he did you. And then you accused him of being a gold-digger. I can't believe you didn't know he was wealthy."

"Just add stupidity to my many flaws."

"I'll say. Here, put some lotion on my back." Mary Leigh handed her a brown bottle and lay on her stomach. "I think this probably happened for the best."

Kathy's hand stopped in mid-stroke. "Lady, you've been out in the sun too long."

"Listen to me. You've been losing weight because Devon wanted you to. The money was just a secondary reason am I right?"

Kathy thought about the question for a few minutes. "Well . . . yes."

"Then you're going about it all wrong." Mary Leigh raised up on her elbows. "Look at the burden you placed on Devon's shoulders. He was like a crutch to you. You depended on him to tell you when to exercise and what to eat. And when the prop was taken away you crumbled. Am I right?"

"More than I like to admit," Kathy agreed wryly. "You're making me see things in a different light." She screwed the top on the brown bottle. "What do you suggest?"

"Stand on your own two feet. You can't lose weight for me or Devon. The only person you need to please is your-self, and by learning to like the person you are, you'll get rid of all these doubts. Then you will find the peace you're looking for. And only then can relax and enjoy Devon."

"Have you thought about becoming a shrink?" Kathy teased.

"No, but I've been told I'd make a darn good bartender."

"Do you suppose it's too late for me and Devon?"

"No. But I think you're going to have to fight to win him back. I don't think he'll make it easy."

"A few months ago I would have given up. But you're right. I'm going to lose that weight for myself and because it was one of my aunt's, I mean my mother's, last wishes. That much I can do for her and of course myself. And if Mr. York still refuses to see me, I'll wait until December where he'll have to meet me face to face. I'll make him listen. And if he doesn't love me, I'll walk away like a lady."

Mary Leigh reached out and patted Kathy on the back. "That's a girl."

"That did sound good. And I do feel better and stronger, but . . ." A sad look crept into Kathy's eyes. "If Devon walks out on me, he'll take my heart with him."

DEVON SAT at his Chippendale desk. He could have sworn he heard his heart beating a moment ago; the stillness seemed to surround and smother him. He really didn't feel like sifting through this stack of papers, but he didn't want to stay at Ed's either. Thanksgiving was a time for family, and Devon felt like an outsider intruding on friends, especially since it was an American custom. He probably should have flown home to visit his parents. He was long overdue, but he didn't want to do that either.

Flipping through the stack of mail, he saw a letter from Kathy. He held it up and stared at the bold, black script much like the lady who had written the note.

Why hadn't she trusted him when he'd given her no cause for doubt? He'd been more than open with her -- more than he had with any woman. And she had the nerve to think he wanted the money. She couldn't have been more insulting.

Didn't she know that he was well off himself? How did she think he got Bridgewell . . . on a credit card? Devon sat thumping the letter on the desk. Perhaps, Katherine didn't know, but the fact still remained, she should have trusted him. He held the envelope to his nose and breathed in her perfume. His throat tightened when he felt a lump held between the confines of the paper. His brows drew together in puzzlement.

Tearing open the envelope, a gold key fell out and hit his desktop. "Bloody hell!" he swore as he read the note. He picked up the key and held it in his palm. "So she thinks she means nothing to me . . . Hell, I was going to ask her to be my wife. Would I ask someone I didn't love?" He threw the half-read note down on his desk and laid the key on it. Maybe he'd read the rest of the note later when he could concentrate, but for now he was in no mood. What he needed was a good workout at the gym . . . something to get his mind off *her*.

AT THE CLUB, Devon worked on each machine with a vengeance. He even set a record on the treadmill. Now, he intended to swim laps in the pool and cool down his body and temper.

He was just getting ready to walk out of the men's dressing room when he heard his name mentioned. He stopped and leaned up against the wall.

"So you think you have a chance to get Devon back?"

"Now that I have the other little bitch out of the way I do," Whitney replied. "Hand me that towel."

"I can't believe that she thought Devon was broke and down on his luck."

Whitney chuckled. "It just takes planting the right gossip."

Devon waited until the women moved away. "So Kathy's doubts had been planted." He drew his brows together. This puts a very interesting light on the whole situation.

CHAPTER 14

*A*s Kathy drove home from the airport, she noticed New Orleans had been dressed in its Christmas finery. All the black light posts wore green wreaths and bright red bows. She turned on the car radio in time to hear that Santa would arrive the following Saturday at noon. Smiling, she could picture all the excited children who would stand in line waiting to tell Santa what they wanted for Christmas. Her favorite holiday outing always was the Yuletide shopping trip to Canal Place Shopping Center. They always had a magnificent thirty-foot Christmas tree complete with a multitude of lights. She might even get desperate enough to sit on Santa's knee herself.

Kathy unlocked the front door and dropped her luggage. A feeling of home ran through her as she breathed in the familiar smells. Sticking her head back outside, she checked the mailbox and pulled out a handful of letters. She gave the door a shove with her foot and headed for the kitchen.

Dropping the mail on the counter, she sorted through

the junk until she saw a letter from the Wildlife Commission. She wasted little time opening the envelope. This had to be her first paycheck. She pulled out the voucher and gasped at the amount. The payment for only two of her paintings had brought six thousand dollars. Never in her wildest dreams had she expected to make that kind of money for *her* paintings.

She could thank Devon for making the contact that landed her the job. Funny, all the good things that had happened in her life lately had something to do with Devon.

Glancing over at her answering machine, she saw a blinking red light. She held her breath in anticipation and pressed the button. "Kathy this is Tina -- your sister -- remember me? Probably not since I haven't heard from you in ages. Give me a call." There was another beep then silence as the recorder rewound.

Kathy let out her breath with a sigh. Devon hadn't called. Evidently, her letter hadn't meant a thing. She picked up the phone and dialed Tina's number. It had been a long time since she'd talked to her sister.

"Hello."

"Hi, you left a message for me."

"Well it's about time," Tina snapped. "Where have you been?"

"I went to Weatherford for Thanksgiving. What did you do?"

She heard Tina blow out her breath. "I spent the holidays by myself."

"What happened to your hunk?"

"The hunk, I found out, was married."

"I guess there's a creep or two under every rock. I'm sorry, Tina, but it's better you found out early before you got too involved with him. I know how much it hurts." Kathy murmured. *Oh, now I know.*

"I guess so." Tina's voice broke miserably. "I had planned on having you over for Thanksgiving, and you spoiled that, too."

"I'm not a mind reader," Kathy said. Her sympathy quickly changed to annoyance with her sister's complaining. "You should have said something."

"By the way, I bumped into Devon yesterday and he wanted to know how you were doing. I was floored. I asked him why he didn't know. He said you two had broken up. What did you do to screw things up this time? Or did he just dump you?"

Kathy almost laughed. Where Tina's comments used to bother her they suddenly had little effect on her. "Let's just say it was a difference of opinion."

"Well I thought you might need a shoulder to cry on."

"No, Tina . . . I don't," Kathy said calmly and hung up the receiver. Then she laughed at her new-found independence. That should put her sister's tail feathers in a twist. When had she ever had the last word on Tina?

Kathy poured herself a cool drink. As she stood at the bar sipping tea, she listened to the silence that surrounded her. Mary Leigh had made everything seem all right, if only for a little while. But back in her home, memories besieged her. Kathy glanced at the kitchen table. She could picture Devon sitting there teasing her and making her laugh at life in general.

There had been love in his eyes then. Now she wasn't so sure he had ever loved her. The night they argued was replayed vividly in her mind. The worst part was she'd brought this misery on herself. With all her doubts, she'd never given Devon much of a chance. Since he hadn't contacted her, he must have figured out he'd made a big mistake and that hurt. Kathy took a swallow of tea to forestall her threatening tears. One way or the other, she had to chase those memories from her head.

If there were going to be a first step now, Devon would have to make it. Kathy was through calling him. She had apologized in the letter, and that's all she could do. Setting the tea glass in the sink, she went to get her luggage.

Climbing the stairs, her life suddenly seemed cold and empty, but time had a way of healing one's wounds. She would survive . . . She would survive!

THE SECOND WEEK of December brought another important letter from the Wildlife Department. One of their clients wanted Kathy to paint a picture of the French Quarters complete with a horse-drawn carriage. Kathy saw no problem with such a request. Her eyes scanned the rest of the letter, but soon she stopped reading and her eyes grew wide. Someone had made a mistake in the price, and she wasted little time in calling her boss, Mr. Gladden.

Kathy skipped all the pleasantries when he answered the phone. "I've just received your letter, and I'm flattered. But there has been a mistake."

"Hello, Kathy," he said in his slow methodical way. "What kind of mistake?"

"Your secretary erroneously typed five thousand dollars instead of a thousand. I just wanted to draw your attention to the mistake and ask when would you like the painting completed."

"I appreciate your call, Kathy. Honesty is a rare thing this day and time, and I enjoy any chance I get to talk to you, however, there has been no mistake. A friend of the Wildlife Department is willing to pay you five thousand dollars. He wants a large painting to go over his fireplace."

"Who is this friend, may I ask?"

"He is one of our benefactors, but I'm afraid he wishes to remain anonymous."

"But why me? He could have someone famous for that amount of money."

"He saw your painting of the Birds in Flight which, by the way, the post office is looking into using on a stamp, and he thought it was full of life and reality and, as he put it, just what he was looking for. It seems your paintbrushes bring magical life to the things they touch."

In that case, Kathy thought, she'd paint a portrait and crawl into it. "I'm glad you're so pleased with my work, Mr. Gladden," she said, brushing off his praise. "I'll get to work on the picture. When does Mr. X want his painting?"

She heard her boss chuckle. "By Christmas. I hope you can take on this assignment on such short notice. I know how busy it can be around the holidays."

Kathy wanted to laugh at his apology. If only he knew, she didn't have anything to do, and the only party she would be attending was on Christmas Eve. "It's no problem. For five thousand dollars, I'll hang the picture for him, too."

KATHY HAD BEEN KEEPING in touch with Jack. He always had a way of making her laugh. Today he and his girlfriend, Sue, were coming over for lunch and then they all would be going Christmas shopping.

"That was a super meal, Kat," Jack said as he helped her and Sue into his blue van and shut the door.

"It wasn't anything." Kathy fastened her seatbelt. "I'm glad you brought the van. I need to go by the art supply store to get a canvas if you don't mind."

"No problem." Jack smiled. "I need to get some supplies myself."

Sue remained in the van, while Kathy and Jack went in for their supplies. It didn't take long before Kathy spotted the canvas she would need. She was glad Jack had accompanied her.

Kathy walked out carrying the front of the canvas and Jack toting the back. She chuckled at Jack's grumblings.

"Doing things big these days huh, Kat." Jack shoved the canvas into the van.

"Only this one. You wouldn't believe what I'm getting paid to paint one picture." She held up her finger.

He shut the rear door of the van and they walked around to the side and climbed in. "Maybe you made the right decision by breaking out on your own. By the time you're rich and famous, I'll still be slaving away at the same old desk, doing the same old job, but at least I will be able to say, I knew Kathy Taylor. She used to sit across from me."

Sue joined in their conversation. "All kidding aside. I've seen your work and it's very good." Her eyes cut to Jack and she laughed at his strange look. "Not that your work isn't good, Jack."

Kathy started laughing with Sue as Jack begrudgingly mumbled, "Gee, thanks."

The rest of the day was spent Christmas shopping. They all agreed to go their separate ways then meet back at Spin, the record store.

Kathy looked at her watch. She couldn't have finished this much ahead of time. But then, she didn't have that many people to buy for. She had gotten Jack and Sue a present, and of course her parents, who were still in England. Now she needed a gift for Tina. After all, it was Christmas and time to put their differences aside.

Kathy arrived at the record store early and decided to browse and find her sister some beach music. Humming the Beach Boy's tune *Rhonda*, she thumbed through the CD's until she finally found the perfect one, an old recording, that Tina had wanted but couldn't find. Picking up the plastic disk, she turned to find a clerk and bumped into someone else.

"Excuse me." Kathy looked up at the man and gasped. Not just any man . . . "Devon."

He had grabbed her arms to keep her from falling. "Kathy."

My God, he was touching her, he was here, and she couldn't stop her heart from slamming against her chest. "W--what are you doing here?"

"I came in to get a CD. How are you doing?"

Of all the questions he could have asked that was the wrong one. "Do you really care?" she snapped.

Evidently, he realized he was still holding her because he immediately dropped his hands as if he burned them. "Certainly, I do."

"Well you have a funny way of showing it." Kathy was getting ready to say more, but Jack walked up and put his arm around her.

"Ready to go, Kat?"

"Y--Yes. Let me pay for this." Kathy glanced at Jack then back to Devon who had stopped looking at her to stare at Jack. It wasn't a very friendly glare. "Nice to see you, Devon." Kathy moved past him to the cash register, but she heard his response.

"I'll see you Christmas Eve, Luv."

Kathy's hands were shaking so much she wasn't sure the clerk had given her the correct change. Had he said Luv?

Kathy managed to walk out of the store without tripping or causing herself any further embarrassment. She found Jack waiting for her by the fountain outside the store. She also resisted the urge to look back at Devon. *God, how she wanted to run back and throw her arms around his neck.* If he would just hold her a few minutes and tell her everything would be fine. It would be all the Christmas she would ever need.

"Would you like to tell me what that was all about?" she asked Jack in a furious whisper. "And where is Sue?"

"Come on." They started through the mall. "Sue is bringing the van around. I thought I'd give you a little help back there."

"A little help? I don't understand. How did you know who he was?"

"For one thing your face was sheet-white and your voice was a little too loud."

"Devon was getting ready to give me some answers to my questions, but you walked up. Devon assumed you were my date, and you did nothing to dissuade him," she accused.

"He sure did." Jack laughed.

She halted abruptly and caught his elbow. "Well, I'm glad to see you can laugh because my problem just got worse."

He shook his head. "Kat, you don't get it do you?"

"Evidently not."

"The man was jealous." Jack took her arm and pulled Kathy along. "Didn't you see his expression when I put my arm around you? I'm sure glad he didn't have a gun."

"He was jealous?" An unexpected warmth filled her body. "He looked angry to me."

"It was green-eyed jealously, Kat! And he wouldn't react that way if he didn't still love you."

They moved through the door to the van. Jack opened the door so Kathy could get in. "Then why is he acting so strange?"

"I don't know, Kat. Only Devon can answer that question."

KATHY LAY in her bed and stared up at the dark ceiling. She could kick herself for not being more blunt. Why hadn't she shrugged away from Jack and demanded to know why Devon had not returned her phone calls? She sighed for the hundredth time. What she really wanted to say was, "Hold me, Devon."

Now she'd have to wait until Christmas Eve. Then she would handle things differently. She'd demand answers to her questions. Jack had said Devon still loved her. She sure hoped Jack was correct.

Kathy got up early the next morning to start on her painting. She began by filling in the background with rich earth-tones and charcoal-grays. By mid-afternoon the buildings and streets were coming alive as she added the tiny lines of the wrought-ironwork on the balustrades.

She cleaned her paintbrush then rubbed the back of her neck. This landscape was challenging because she'd never done anything this large. She glanced at her watch.

She'd start again tomorrow, but for now, she needed to get ready for Tina's first dinner visit.

"Look at you, you look great!" Tina hugged Kathy.

Kathy hid her surprise at her sister's compliment, attributing Tina's mood to Christmas spirit.

"Where is your Christmas tree?" Tina asked as she followed Kathy to the kitchen.

"I didn't get one. I'm just not in the mood."

"That doesn't sound like you."

"I know." Kathy shrugged. "Things are different this Christmas, and I'm feeling kind of down."

"I know what you mean," Tina agreed. "Men sure can screw things up, can't they?"

"I don't know," Kathy laughed. "I don't do too bad a job myself." She decided to change the subject. Picking up a potholder, she opened the oven door and pulled out a pan. "I hope you are hungry. I've fixed marinated chicken and baked potatoes."

"That sounds good." Tina picked up the plates and took them to the table.

They talked about small things during dinner, and Kathy learned that while she was gone her parents had tried to phone to tell her they were going to France before returning home. Kathy listened to Tina talking about her work while her own mind drifted as always to Devon and the many dinners they had shared together. Kathy moved her food around on her plate, eating very little. Somehow food didn't taste as good as usual.

After dinner they went to the living room and

exchanged presents. Tina handed a big silver package to Kathy.

She tore off the paper and pulled out a Kelly Green sweater in a size XL. "Don't you think this is a little big?" she asked her eyebrow arching in question.

Tina started laughing. "I guess it is, but I never thought you'd lose the weight."

"Me neither, but I do admit, I feel much better."

Tina picked up her glass of wine. "I'd like to make a toast." Kathy reached for her glass, then Tina continued. "I know I've been a jerk over the years, but now I have had a lot of time alone to think things over. I guess what I'm trying to say is, I'm sorry, and I've missed you these past few months. Here's to a Merry Christmas and a better year for both of us." Tina managed to choke out as tears well up in her eyes.

Kathy smiled at her sister's tears. For once in Tina's life she seemed sincere, and Kathy couldn't believe her sister was crying over her. This had been a strange Christmas indeed. "Thank you," she said graciously as she stood. "I've got something to show you."

In a few minutes, Kathy returned with her birth certificate. "Look at this."

Tina scanned the document. "It's your birth certificate. Why are you showing it to me?"

"Take a look at the mother."

Tina's eyes widened. "Aunt Catherine! She was your mother?"

Kathy noted the surprise in Tina's features. So that answered one question. Tina didn't know. "That's the way it appears. I now know why she left so much to me."

"So we're cousins instead of sisters?"

Kathy shook the birth certificate. "According to this slip of paper."

"Now all the attention from Aunt Catherine makes sense. I don't know about how you feel, but as far as I'm concerned we've been through too much to be cousins. You're my sister, and I'm yours. Providing you still want me."

"I think we've both changed." Kathy lifted her glass toward Tina. "Here's to growing older and hopefully wiser."

IN THE DAYS BEFORE CHRISTMAS, the painting became Kathy's obsession. She poured her heart and soul into each stroke. The buildings took on character and one could almost see the sparkle in the eyes of the people both old and young on the sidewalks.

Finally, she signed her name and cleaned her brush. Moving to the door, she reached for the light switch, but instead of flipping it off she turned to look one more time at her landscape.

"It's beautiful," she whispered. She knew it had to be her finest work, but until now she didn't know why.

The picture depicted two lovers in a horse drawn carriage going through the streets of the Vieux Carrè. She could almost imagine the man reaching into his pocket and pulling out a necklace. Tears sneaked down her cheeks and puddled on her chin. She'd managed to capture the best night of her life . . . the night when Devon had freely given her his love.

With a shake of her head, she turned off the light and

shut the door. If only she could turn back the clock. There always seemed to be too many 'ifs' in her life.

Would the owner of the painting ever know how precious this picture was to her? Would the painting capture his heart on lonely nights when he sits in front of his fireplace and gazes at the painting? Will he know it's a moment in time captured but never forgotten?

Memories . . . all she had were memories . . .

CHAPTER 15

The clock radio clicked on precisely at seven o'clock and music began to play. It took a few minutes before Kathy heard the tune of Jingle Bells, ringing in her ears.

She stretched her hands over her head, and her eyes fluttered opened. Christmas Eve had arrived. Where had the last six months gone? It seemed just the other day she'd walked into Devon's office and made a fool of herself, which always seemed the case when he was near her.

Slowly, she let the last six months tumble through her mind. When she looked at the clock again it was eight o'clock and time to start the day. One way or the other, she had a feeling this wouldn't be a day she'd soon forget.

Kathy had just finished breakfast when the doorbell chimed. Getting up, she put the dishes in the sink and wondered who it could be so early in the morning. She finished washing her hands and went to the door.

A young boy dressed in a gray uniform stood on the porch with a garment bag slung over his back. "Good morning. I have a delivery for Miss Taylor."

"I'm Miss Taylor."

He handed her a clipboard. "Sign here." He pointed to the line numbered twenty-five.

When she handed him back his papers, he whipped the garment bag around and handed it to her. He tipped his hat. "Merry Christmas."

"Was there a message?" She stopped him as he walked down the sidewalk.

"Afraid not, ma'am."

"Thank you." Kathy closed the door, feeling a little let down. But then what had she expected . . . the man hadn't spoken to her in weeks. "Oh, well," she sighed as she climbed the stairs to her bedroom.

She hung the garment bag on the closet door. "So the dress has arrived." She stood staring at the bag, daring herself to open it. Now the question was, had she lost the weight required to wear the gown? She bit her lip as she stared at intimidating sack. "We'll find out tonight." There wasn't a lot she could do if the dress didn't fit. Besides, she had bought an alternate dress just in case.

By midmorning, Kathy found herself cheerful for the first time in weeks. She hummed Christmas carols as she cleaned the house. After checking the painting to make sure it was dry, she brought it downstairs and propped it against the back of the couch.

She stared at her masterpiece. Did she really want to part with it? Rubbing her chin, she walked around the living room and stared at the walls. There wasn't one wall that would accommodate such a large picture, so she called her boss and told him to send a van for the painting. Maybe one day she'd paint another for herself.

As the afternoon dragged by, Kathy found her nervousness increasing. This was the day she'd waited for, yet dreaded at the same time. She found herself shampooing carpets, cleaning out the refrigerator, mopping the floors.

Anything to keep busy.

THE DOORBELL RANG precisely at seven pm. "Jack is prompt tonight when he has been late all his life," Kathy mumbled as she made her way to the door, pinning up her last hot curler.

She opened the door and her eyes grew wide. Dressed in a white Tux stood a man that resembled Jack. "Is that really you in there?" Kathy joked and motioned for him to come in.

He laughed and swept past her. "Yeah, Kat. It's me." Jack put his hands on his lapel and turned for her inspection. "Not bad, huh?"

"You look great. I don't think I've ever seen you dressed up before."

Jack frowned. "Speaking of being dressed . . . Why aren't you ready? I don't think they'll let you in the place in a bathrobe even if you are the guest of honor."

"I know, I know." Kathy started to pace. "But I'm so nervous. And everything has gone wrong." Suddenly, she twirled around and pointed to her face. "Look at this! I smeared my mascara and my hair looks a fright. I can't hang onto anything. And I don't have the slightest idea if the dress will fit."

She lifted her arms and let them fall to her side. "I just can't do this, Jack." She sank in the nearest chair. "The moment of truth is here. The dress was delivered this afternoon."

Jack walked over, took her hand, and pulled her up.

"What you've got, Kat, is a bundle of nerves." Putting his arm around her, he escorted her to the liquor cabinet. "I've got just the thing for you."

"Oh, that's great!" Her last thread of composure slipped and her voice cracked. "My whole life is falling apart, and you want me to get drunk so I can make a complete fool out of myself. I've got news for you, I don't need liquor for that, I do a pretty good job without it."

"My, my aren't we sarcastic tonight." Jack poured her a splash of brandy. "I don't want you to get drunk. I just want you to calm down, so I don't have to put that damn dress on you, myself. Here, drink this." He handed her the glass. "Believe me it will work and if it doesn't we'll try a hammer to knock some sense into your head."

Kathy smiled, held her breath, and swallowed the golden liquor. She immediately felt the warmth spread over her body.

"You still with me, Kat?" Jack patted her on the back.

She coughed, sputtered and finally nodded. "I do feel better."

"Good. Now I want you to go up those stairs." He pointed. "And get dressed. We have a party to attend and your carriage awaits."

Kathy went back to her room where she once again attempted to put on her makeup. Finally, when she was satisfied, she added the finishing touch. She brushed her face and shoulders with a gold-iridescent powder.

She took the curlers out of her hair then tilted her head over and back-brushed her long chestnut-colored hair. "Okay hair, it's now or never." She stood up and shook her head watching her wavy hair fall midway down her back. Good. Kathy grabbed the hair spray and sprayed her locks before anything could move. Then she took the shimmering powder and swished the gold dust through her hair.

She might not be as pretty as Whitney, but she was going to do her damnedest to make Devon take a second look at her tonight. Would he bring Whitney tonight or would he come alone? Kathy knew she would have at least one chance. For appearance sake, he would have to dance one dance with her.

Her stomach fluttered at the thought of being in his arms again. "Damn it!" she swore, hitting her fist on the counter. He loved her! He was just being stubborn.

She turned to face the garment bag. Now was the time. She found her stomach quivering as she moved toward the unknown. Slowly, she unzipped the bag, thinking of the first time she had laid eyes on the dress. So much had happened since then, so much had changed. Kathy had to admit she was a different person both inside and out. Even if this dress didn't fit, some good had come out of the last few months. But then she had a feeling that's what Aunt Catherine intended.

Grasping the black sequined material, she slowly pulled it out of the bag. The sequins winked at her like a thousand tiny diamonds, then her gaze came to a halt. There pinned to the top was a note.

Her fingers shook as she took the pin out and unfolded the letter. She recognized Devon's handwriting immediately.

Good luck, Kathy.
Don't be late.
Devon

Kathy frowned as she looked on the back. "Is that all

he had to say?" Then again it was more than he'd said to her since the fight. Was this a sign? Or was she just being hopeful?

Hell, she didn't know. And she was tired of trying to figure everything out. What would happen would happen.

"Please let it fit." She unzipped the garment and prepared to slip into the gown.

She held her breath and prayed it would go over her hips. Shutting her eyes, she tugged the material up over her hips then reached behind her and grasped the zipper and pulled. It moved slowly then stopped. "Oh God, it doesn't fit!" Kathy moaned.

Her eyes popped open and she pulled the dress to her front so she could see the problem. Slowly, letting out her breath, she discovered the zipper hung on a tiny piece of material. She fixed the problem and twisted the gown back in position. Again she closed her eyes, sucked in her stomach, said a little prayer, and eased the zipper up. When she opened them again the dress was on.

It fit!

She had done it.

She was rich.

So why wasn't she happy? Kathy definitely knew the answer to that question. Wealth couldn't buy the happiness she sought.

"Are you about ready, Kat?" Jack shouted from downstairs.

"I'm coming," Kathy yelled as she turned back toward the mirror. She marveled at the perfect fit. Aunt Catherine had know all the time. Kathy walked back and forth. The strapless gown clung to her perfectly. With every step she took her black silk-stockinged leg peeked from beneath the long crepe skirt.

Before going down stairs, Kathy took a final look in the mirror. She didn't see the elegant young lady she'd become; instead she saw a red bump that was threatening to break out on the end of her nose.

After tonight, she was going to buy a new mirror!

"I'm ready," Kathy said as she walked down the stairs.

"Damn if you won't be the queen of the ball," Jack all but shouted. "I'll have to fight the men away from you -- providing you want me to, that is." He took her hand and placed it in the crook of arm. "But if we don't hurry our coach is likely to turn back into a pumpkin."

Kathy bit her fingernails as they drove across town through the bright Christmas lights. What seemed like an eternity was only a short ride and soon they were there.

Jack swung the car into a reserve parking spot, then walked around and opened the door for Kathy. She had her head rested on the headrest. Turning, she put her feet on the ground and then looked up. "Jack."

"Yes."

"I'm going to puke."

Jack chuckled then declared, "No you're not." He pulled her up on her feet. "You're going to square these shoulders, and we're going through that door with your head held high. Just keep reminding yourself that as of tonight you're wealthier than half those people in there.

"But I'd give up every cent for Devon."

"I know, Kat, I know."

KATHY STOOD straight with her hand lightly resting on Jack's arm. She was very thankful he'd agreed to accompany her tonight. Sue had been so understanding. They stood on the top step that descended to a grand ballroom.

Soft music played in the crowded, noisy room. There had to be at least six hundred men and women gathered here. Kathy looked straight ahead and went down the steps never giving the first indication she was nervous.

She wasn't sure what she should to do since she didn't know any of these people. A shout of laughter caught her attention and she turned, but didn't recognize anyone in the group so they couldn't be laughing at her. She tugged on Jack's arm and whispered. "Do you know any of these people?"

Jack lowered his head. "No Kat, I don't recall seeing any of them at the bowling alley before." He chuckled.

"I wonder if Devon has arrived?"

Devon spotted Kathy the minute she entered the ballroom. His eyes followed her across the room. Damn, she was a real beauty tonight. Her long, thick hair caressed her shoulders and the top of her breasts, and seemed to shimmer with every move she made.

She had achieved her goal and that made him smile because she had done it on her own. When the chips had been stacked against her, Kathy had prevailed. She appeared regal and enticingly beautiful. A wave of pride swept through him.

He sipped his drink and watched her over the rim of the glass. Somehow her smile lacked its usual sparkle and his heart ached, knowing he'd been the cause. Her infectious wit was one of the things he loved about her most. He'd never laughed so much as when Kathy had been with him. Drawing his gaze away from the face that haunted her dreams, he noticed Kathy's male companion. *Who the hell is that,* he wondered, then he remembered it was the man he'd seen with her at the record store.

He'd been through hell these last few weeks. Evidently, she hadn't given him a second thought. What did that note she'd sent him say? He drew his brows together. The only thing he could remember were the words "I'm sorry". Damn, he wished now he'd gone back and reread the entire note, but as soon as the key dropped from the envelope his anger had taken over.

It was about time they got a few things straight.

"I'M GOING to get us some champagne, Kat. Will you be okay until I get back?"

Kathy looked at Jack and smiled. What would she do without him? "I'll try not to faint while you're gone."

Jack had no more than walked away when Kathy spotted Devon coming her way. The word magnificence popped into her mind. His black jacket and trousers appeared to be tailor-made just for him. A snowy white shirt peeked out from beneath his tux and made his tanned features all the more breathtakingly handsome.

She stared in a very unladylike fashion, her eyes never leaving his. But she didn't understand what she saw. He appeared to be angry.

"Hello, Devon."

"Congratulations, I see you have accomplished your goal."

"You doubted I would?"

"No, Luv. I never had any doubts, but I believe you did."

She watched to see if he was making fun of her, but his harsh lines had softened. The anger she saw earlier had disappeared. Smiling, she nodded. "Yes, I did doubt myself." She held her hands out away from her sides. "What do you think?"

"I think you are very beautiful." He reached up and let the back of his fingers travel down the side of her face. "But then you've always been beautiful to me." The sincerity in Devon's voice took Kathy's breath and made her knees grow weak.

"Why haven't you called?" she whispered, barely able to get out the words. His gentle touch hadn't left her unaffected.

"I believe you made it clear you didn't trust me and the only way --"

"Here's your champagne, Kat." Jack handed her a glass.

Jack had the damnedest habit of showing up at the wrong time, Kathy thought irritably. But she smiled instead of biting off his head and reached for the glass. "Thank you. Jack, I'd like for you to meet Devon York."

"Devon, this is a friend of mine, Jack Walker."

"Pleasure," Devon snapped out before looking back to her. "Are you ready to present the Dubois Award?"

Kathy nodded and Devon guided her toward the bandstand. "I'll start off with the formalities and then turn the actual presentation over to you." He stared at her and evidently saw how nervous she'd become. Squeezing her hand he said, "There is nothing to this. It will be over in a few minutes."

She moistened her lips, but she couldn't quit staring at

him. *I love you, Devon.* She implored with her eyes. *Please give me a sign that you love me, too.* He had such a remote look that it scared her. After several moments she found her voice. "I'll be fine, but I would like to speak with you later."

"Perhaps there will be time," he said bluntly, and Kathy's heart sank. Was it too late? Had she lost him through her foolishness? She should have demanded to see him the very next day. Instead, she'd waited until the sore festered. Now things were worse.

Devon cleared his throat and drew everyone's attention. "Ladies and Gentlemen," he began his speech, speaking with such ease and grace. Kathy wondered if anyone else thought he was the most stunning man she'd ever met. Dressed in his tuxedo, he appeared the elegant nobleman in every aspect. She heard little of what he said until he turned and held out his hand to her.

"May I present Katherine Taylor, Mrs. Dubois' niece."

She squared her shoulders and stepped up to the microphone. "I'm sorry my aunt cannot be here to give out the prestigious award tonight. I believe this was her favorite time of year. And I now know why this time of year is special to me, too. This year the Dubois award goes to Helen Clark." Kathy waited for the applause to die down and watched as Helen made her way to the platform. "Helen has established a school to teach underprivileged children to read." Kathy shook Helen's hand and handed her the plaque and an envelope.

After the recipient made a short speech, Devon stepped back to the microphone. "Ladies and Gentlemen, as is the custom, I'd like to start off the first dance. Please feel free to join us."

Kathy saw Devon reach out his hand. "I believe this is our dance." They moved to the center of the floor where

Devon swept her into his arms just as the orchestra began a waltz.

"You handled that very well, m'lady."

Kathy smiled remembering another time they played the same game. "Thank you, kind sir. I must say you are a marvelous dancer."

He nodded his head at the compliment. "I do think, though, you are much too far away." He pulled her next to his long frame never missing a single step.

Kathy's heart leaped at the closeness of their bodies, but she didn't let on her feelings. Instead she replied impishly, "Yes, I believe this is much better."

"I hope this doesn't upset your boyfriend."

"My what?"

"I believe you called him Jack," Devon snapped. "And I must say you didn't waste much time replacing me."

Kathy saw the anger in Devon's eyes. Jack had been right. "I do believe you're jealous."

"And rightly so. I thought we had something, Kathy."

Kathy noted that a few other couples had joined them on the dance floor, but she managed to hold her voice down even though she wanted to shout. "You pompous, ass." she hissed. "How dare you judge me when you've had Whitney clinging all over you."

"I've not dated her since before I met you," he shot back. "Except to take her out to eat, and that was at my partners' insistence. But then, as I recall, you didn't want to hear any explanations."

Kathy felt as if she'd been slapped. It had been nothing like she thought, but before she could reply the music ended.

"I need to speak to some other guests, excuse me," Devon announced coldly. He reached in his pocket and pulled out an envelope. "Your aunt asked that I give this to you after you made your goal." He placed the letter in her hand and left her standing in the middle of the floor.

Kathy had to get out of here. Her eyes traveled the room until she spied a set of double French doors leading to a terrace. Maybe the fresh air would help her to think straight. She made her way through the crowd, and grabbed a glass of champagne as she passed the refreshments table. Just before she opened the door, she looked back and saw Jack entertaining himself with several ladies.

The cool air felt good on Kathy's warm cheeks. Had she screwed everything up again? Every time she got close something would happen to send things back the wrong way. She promised herself she'd never mention the name Whitney again.

Tearing open the envelope, she pulled out a letter and opened it. The light was dim where she stood, but light enough she could make out the words.

> *Kathy,*
> *Somehow I know you'll have made your goal*
> *because you are so much like me.*
> *By now, I'm sure you've gone through my personal*
> *belongings and have found your birth certificate.*
> *How many times I longed to tell you that you were*
> *my daughter. I want you to know, I didn't give*
> *you up because I did not love you, but because it*
> *wasn't fair for you to grow up with an old*
> *codger like me. I was a widow who'd been*
> *alone too long when you were born, and I didn't*
> *want accusations to hang over your head. People*
> *can be so cruel, Katherine, I hope you never*
> *have to suffer.*

*Since I couldn't do much when you were growing up
except to watch over you. I have now provided
you with enough money for you to live
comfortably. I hope I've also provided you with
a husband. You can find no finer man than
Devon. From the time I met him, I knew he
was the man for you.*

*Remember no matter what happens, I have loved you
from the very first breath you took and I'm very
proud of you, darling.*

Love,
Mother

KATHY'S THROAT tightened and her eyes burned as she stared out into the darkness. "Aunt Catherine . . . or should I say Mother, I've sure made a mess of things." Kathy drank the rest of her champagne. "If only I had your wisdom and courage, then I would know what to do now."

DEVON'S ANGER eased as he spoke with several of his acquaintances. Then he spotted Jack speaking with two women and immediately his jaw tightened. The ladies were just telling Jack goodbye when Devon walked up.

"Kathy isn't enough that you needed two more?" he said in a voice of tightly controlled anger.

Instead of getting angry as Devon expected him to do, the fool smiled at him. "You know, I've never believed the saying, 'Love is blind.' But in your case I'd say the saying is dead on the money."

"I beg your pardon." Devon looked at the fool, puzzled.

"I'm only a friend of Kathy's. I am the shoulder she's been crying on while you've done a pretty good job of breaking her heart. If you both would quit jumping to wrong conclusions and open your eyes, you might find out you love each other very much."

"Just a friend, you say." Devon ran his hand through his hair. He remained quiet for a few minutes, but when he looked at Jack again Devon was smiling. He reached over and patted him on the back. "I think you've been a damn good friend to her, and I appreciate that. Where is she? I believe we've some matters to discuss."

"She went through those doors about ten minutes ago." Jack pointed and grinned.

Devon could see Kathy leaning against the rail and staring out into the darkness. The cool wind whipped her long strands of hair around her bare shoulders and he saw her shiver from the cold. The little fool, he thought as he removed his jacket.

Walking up behind her, he draped the garment over her shoulders. She jumped but relaxed as soon as she realized who it was. Again she stared out into the darkness.

"Have you found any answers out there?" Devon murmured before turning her to face him.

He saw the tears shimmering on her eyelashes and the letter clutched tightly in her hand. "Did the letter distress you, Luv?"

She didn't say anything but handed him the paper.

Devon quickly read the note. "Bloody hell! Catherine was your mother?"

He saw Kathy nod. "I should have known." He smiled. "There are many things that are alike in both of you." Devon began to worry because Kathy had yet to speak. He gave her a slight shake. "Why haven't you said anything?"

Kathy swallowed then took the tip of her tongue and wet her lips before she spoke. "Where you are concerned, Devon, I can't seem to say the right things." Her voice shook. "I don't want to fight anymore. I'm sorry I accused you falsely."

He placed a finger over her lips. "I, too, am sorry. You must believe me, Luv, I never intended to cause you any hurt."

She started to speak, but again he placed a finger over her lips. "Let me finish." He pulled her to him and wrapped his arms around her, resting his chin on her head. "One of the reasons I stayed away these last two months is because I wanted you to see you could make your goal without my help or anyone else's. You've always had it in you, Luv, but you needed to build your confidence. And tonight, when you walked through those doors looking like a queen, I knew you had grown as a person."

Kathy looked up at him and Devon practically melted with the love he saw in her eyes. His mouth came down hungrily on hers. My God, it had been much too long. With her body melting into his, he possessively pulled her hips toward him and at the same time parted her lips, taking all the sweetness he'd craved over the last lonely months. An aching desire ran through him as her tongue touched his, making him deepen his kiss with a fierce tenderness.

Kathy wanted to cry out with the joy that ran through

her veins as Devon ravished her mouth. He held her as if he thought she might turn and run away from him. *Foolish man*, she thought. Never, no, never again would she leave him.

He held her locked within his embrace as he waited for his breathing to calm down. "I want to show you something," he whispered. "Let's go."

"L--Leave the party. Can we do that?"

"We sure can. Jack knows I'm with you, so you needn't worry about your friend."

"You know Jack?" Kathy blinked. She couldn't believe that Devon knew Jack.

"We had a nice little chat. It was very interesting."

"But what?" Kathy asked but Devon didn't answer.

He walked at a very fast pace, and Kathy ran to keep up with him. "Where are we going?"

"You'll see."

It felt good to climb back into Devon's car. They were soon out of the city and into the country. Kathy couldn't imagine where he was taking her. But she really didn't care just as long as she was with him. Suddenly, he turned onto a familiar road and she saw the covered bridge decorated with Christmas lights. Bridgewell.

"Your house is finished?"

"Yes, Luv it is," he said as he stopped the car at the front door and pressed a button so the lights in the house came on. "I want you to be the first to see it."

She followed Devon into the house but instead of going into the living room he showed her the rest of the place. "This reminds me of a palace, Devon. You must be very proud."

He reached down and kissed her cheek. "Almost as proud as I am of you." He put his hand on her back and guided her to the living room. Before entering he said, "Shut your eyes. I want you to see something."

Kathy laughed. "I'll have a hard time seeing it with my eyes closed."

"You know what I mean." He waited for her to close her lids.

She felt herself being pulled along and then he took her arms and turned her around. "You can open them."

Her hand flew to her mouth. Kathy stood in front of his fireplace where a fire flickered in the hearth. A huge Christmas tree with thousands of sparkling lights stood to the left of the fireplace. But her eyes didn't linger on the leaping flames, they looked above the mantel. There hanging in all its splendor was the painting she'd poured her heart into. "The picture was for you," she whispered and turned to see him smiling at her.

"I wanted to remember that night always. And who better to paint it than the lady I was with." He reached in his pocket and pulled out the key. "I believe you forgot to wear this tonight." The necklace dangled from his fingers as he handed it to her. Kathy took it and Devon turned and walked over to the stereo. "If you only knew how angry it made me when you returned your gift."

"You never said anything," she commented as she fastened the clasp. "I didn't think you cared."

He took her in his arms as Whitney Houston began singing *I'll always love you.*

Kathy rested her cheek on his chest, thinking she'd never felt like this in her entire life. Just maybe Santa had brought her the gift she desired most.

"I can't believe you didn't think I cared," Devon murmured into her hair. "Do you think you'll be happy in this home with me?"

She looked at him. "I'll be happy anywhere you are, Devon. But what if I gain my weight back?"

"Kathy, do you remember the night I made love to you? I didn't make love to a fat woman, nor a thin woman. It was to the woman I loved."

He took her face in his hands and tipped it up, so he could look deeply into her eyes. And then as if cued, the lights dimmed and Devon sang a song that Kathy would remember the rest of her life.

I--I'll . . . I--I'll always love you.

ABOUT THE AUTHOR

All-Star author, Brenda Jernigan is a bestselling author. She writes both contemporary and historical novels. She has been nominated for several awards – Book Seller's Best Award, The Maggie Award, The Holt Medallion Award and a RONE Award.

Publisher's Weekly says, "Brenda Jernigan writes Romance, Adventure and Magic."

She grew up as a tomboy and really had no use for books. It wasn't until she was taking her son to Story Hour at the local library that the librarian gave her a copy of DEVIL'S DESIRE by Laurie McBain. After that Brenda became hooked on historicals. Brenda's first book, THE DUKE'S LADY, was bought and published by Kensington Publishing and her career as a storyteller took off.

"As usual her characters are interesting, her plot action-packed, and her love story filled with conflict and emotion. A great read from a talented writer." **Rendezvous Magazine.**

"The characters had me hooked from the beginning. This book touched my heart and will definitely be one of my recommends for May."
   Cindi Streicher – Waldenbooks
   RWA Bookseller of the Year 2002

Contact Brenda

e-mail - www.bkj1608@juno.com

webpage -www.brendajbooks.com

Facebook - *http://www.facebook.com/bkjbooks*

Follow me on Twitter - https://twitter.com/bkj1608

ALSO BY BRENDA JERNIGAN

AUTHOR'S NOTE

Merry Christmas! Thank you for spending Christmas with me
and Kathy as she made her way to her happily ever after. I hope
you laughed and cried and most of all found love.

May Christmas bring you the greatest gift of all ... Love.

The Ladies Series

THE DUKE'S LADY

LOVE ONLY ONCE

THE WICKED LADY

CHRISTMAS IN CAMELOT

BLACK MAGIC

The Misfit Series

DANCE ON THE WIND

UNTIL SEPTEMBER

WHISPERS ON THE WIND

SEPTEMBER STORM

THE CHOICE

DIAMOND IN THE ROUGH